the Last Good King

Michelle Janene

Based on the screenplay by
David M. Hyde

STRONG TOWER
P R E S S

Sacramento, CA

Strong Tower Press, PO Box 293632, Sacramento, CA 95829
http://strongtowerpress.com

Scriptures are taken from *The Holy Bible: King James Version*. Dallas, TX: Brown Books Publishing, 2004. Print. All rights reserved.

Edited by: Joanna White
Cover Art by: Whetstone Designs
Images: Knight - Dreamstine, Fosters; Forest light - Unsplash, Johannes Plenio; Stirling bridge - Deposit Photos, Alexey.fedoren@gmail.com
Cover Fonts: Aon Cari Celtic - DaFont; Semplicita Pro - Adobe; Arial

ISBN:978-1-942320-39-5

Thank you David, for trusting me with your script.

PROLOGUE

Dolwyddelan, Wales 1283

The wails and groans of the dying were almost enough to drown out the last of the skirmishes around the battlefield. Almost.

King Edward rode past men crawling for help and the dead in a field rife with gore.

"At last, these Welsh dogs have been brought to heel, Your Majesty." his commander, John de Warenne, said as he rode beside him.

"Aye." Edward's gaze swept over the field filled with too many dead English. A hard-fought battle left its mark on land and soul.

John drew Edward's attention from the quieting battlefield. "Llywelyn was a fool. He never should have refused to pay you tribute."

Edward tightened his fist on the reins as he fought to control his rage. "He never should have married the late Simon de Montfort's daughter."

John released a harsh snort. "The man meant to provoke you by parading his alliance with your former kidnappers. You should have killed him then."

As they approached the far side of the battlefield, Edward again looked at the death around him and listened to the wails of the dying. "He's dead now. His greater mistake was trusting his own brother.

Dafydd has been a great asset these last six years."

"If that fool had been content with the land you gifted him, none of this would have been necessary." The creaking of their saddles was drowned out by the still-screaming cries of the wounded men.

Edward glanced at the two towers poking their heads over the curtain wall on the hill. The defenders had fought from the battlements atop the tall wall. Their arrows hurtled endless over the moat below. Dolwyddelan Castle had been Llywelyn's pride when he claimed the title Prince of Wales. As King of England, Edward planned to oversee far grander fortifications erected in order to secure this land against any future revolt.

"Our men have the last of Dafydd's commanders cornered." John pointed to the cluster of men they approached.

Commander Angwyn Kenseth, his captain Inek Ramonth, and another Welshmen stood back-to-back. They circled, lunged, and slashed their swords at Edward's men who enclosed them in a tight ring of swords.

Ramonth was an able fighter; even hemmed in on every side, he deflected two English swords with quick strikes of his own weapon. "Come on then! You coward blackguards!"

Edward and John dismounted as the English soldiers waited. Their captives weren't going anywhere. His men-at-arms made way as Edward and his commander strode toward the Welsh fighters. Their mail rattled as they marched through the circle of Englishmen.

The third Welshman lunged forward. Kenseth tried to arrest the rash action of the young man. The junior soldier didn't make it three strides before John opened his throat and ran him through. The Welshman dropped to the ground as John stepped back beside Edward.

Edward approached the two remaining Welshmen. "Commander, the battle is lost. Your men are lost. Castle Dolwyddelan has fallen." He said the next words with the tiniest bit of sympathy. "Your own son is dead this day."

Kenseth's sword tip lowered by a degree and he swayed on his feet. His captain, Ramonth, seized his arm to steady him.

Edward held Kenseth in a hard stare. "Bow a knee, Commander, before any more need die."

Kenseth's weapon lowered, making his captain turn to face him with his brows arched high. Kenseth now steadied Ramonth with a hand against his captain's chest. With a determined nod, Kenseth thrust his sword in the ground and dropped to one knee.

Edward shifted his gaze to Ramonth. "Captain?"

Ramonth held his chin high and tightened his grip on his blade. At last, he, too, planted it in the blood-drenched soil and descended to his knee.

Kenseth's gaze rose. He may have been defeated, but he was anything but conquered.

Chapter 1

Conwy, Wales 1296

Angwyn Kenseth paused, closed his eyes against the sun's glare, and wiped his brow with his arm before he surveyed his lands again. Llwyn Gwyon was his home now. "Hey-yup." He slapped the reigns on the plow horse in front of him. The horse lumbered forward with a snort as the plow cut through the dirt. It added the scent of rich soil to the stink of his sweat. Two of his workers followed behind him and planted seeds in the tilled soil. The sounds of their amiable chatter was a balm to his soul.

As he neared the end of the field, he lifted his gaze to the eight-towered, white stone monstrosity on the horizon. His overlord, Edward I, was building castles all over Wales and creating holdings that were only for the English. Angwyn didn't know if it was a blessing or a curse that he still held Llwyn Gwyon. Edward had been the cause of his son's death when he had laid waste to Wales. But, in the end, Angwyn had bent a knee to the man to save his own neck and that of his men who had survived.

He sighed and looked back at his workers. Good, honest men. Many of their labors were for none other than Edward and his English hounds now. He was king of England, but, now, he claimed the title of Prince of Wales, too. Which meant he lived in his new castle only a stone's throw from Angwyn's home.

His wife, Gwendolyn, stepped outside their home. She may have been forty-two, but she was still a fine-looking woman with a shapely figure of a much younger woman. The payments to the overlord kept her in simple gowns, though she followed the fashion of covering her head. Gwendolyn had lovely, rich brown hair that was only now starting to gray—unlike his that was half way to being completely gray.

Katlyn, a servant girl, carried the laundry and walked beside Gwendolyn. "Yes, ma'am."

Angwyn clenched and unclenched his fists and turned a hard stare to Conwy Castle again. Something needed to be done. Gwendolyn deserved far better. She deserved her son.

The breeze off the Conwy River ruffled his shirt and brought an unease that settled in his belly.

The sound of charging hooves approached. Gwendolyn and Katlyn hurried out of the way. A messenger raced past the women and reined in beside Angwyn.

Keep in Din Osways, Scotland

Lord Sintest stroked his ratty gray beard and stared out the window at the courtyard where his men milled about. He was sixty-five-years-old, stuck in this perpetually waterlogged, backward land, with ungrateful, uncivilized people. "Rain. Nothing but endless rain. It fuels the rebellious curs of the land. It waters their rage and can't be held." He was a regular in the king's army, not some wet nurse. The king owed him. "I should be commanding armies for His Majesty's glory. Yes, a command worthy of my skill. Not these laze abouts. They are waterlogged, too. Soggy, useless men." A month ago, he'd sent the king a letter saying such. Who knew how long it would take the messenger to get to Edward and return with his new orders? Delayed by rain, the messenger would no doubt claim. Road washed away. Caught a chill.

Oh, this horrid land. Sintest could think of no good reason for the king to want him punished. That was what Scotland was—punishment.

"My lord."

Sintest jumped and gasped. He turned toward the meeting chamber door his guard called through, ready to berate him.

"A messenger has arrived from the king."

Sintest bounced off his heels a little as he clapped his hands. "Good. Come." Surely, his fortunes were about to turn. "My freedom is at hand. Away from this bog. Back to my rightful place," he muttered as the door opened.

A regular in the king's colors strolled into the meeting chamber. He was wet, but clean, and well-groomed. Finally, a man who knew how to be a soldier.

"Well, come on, man, hand it over. What news does Edward send?" He glanced again at the damp surcoat the man wore. His stare deepened, almost drilling into the surcoat of the soldier. "Rain! A scourge on this land. Never stops. Everything is always wet, molding, and mildewed." He huffed as his gaze returned to the message in the man's hand. "Well, man, did you have a letter for me or not?"

The black-haired messenger reached out his hand clamped around a piece of parchment bearing Edward's seal.

Sintest snatched it from the man's grasp. "Go on, out with you. I am more than capable of reading it myself. I'm not an imbecile. Let me be. I'll read it in privacy. Go, man! And take that water with you. Blasted rain. Everything in this land is wretched." He waved his own man out as well.

After another glance out the window at his undisciplined guards blurred by fresh raindrops, Sintest broke the seal and read the message.

By Order of King Edward I King of England and Prince of Wales,

Due to your continued incompetence, you are hereby stripped of your rank and removed from command...

"No favor. Set aside. Forsaken. No. That can't be. This missive is for another. He can't abandon me. Set aside. I won't ..." He shook as he stalked across the front of the chamber. "No, this is not for me." He shook the dismissal in his hand. His hard steps slapped against the stone. "No, I have served faithfully. I am the king's man." Raindrops plinked against the window. "Abandoned ... set aside." His voice grew to a roar and his arms locked straight and shook. "Never! I've serviced as I was told ... He can't toss me aside." Sintest stomped to the hearth and glared at the red glowing embers. "I'll show His Majesty what he can do with his dismissal." He tossed the message inside and watched it smolder over the hot coals. "He's no right! I've served ... Bog ... Rain ... Served ... with weak men ... Rebels that can't ..."

Sintest stepped to his table, his heart thundered in his ears. He glanced at the signet ring that gave him the right to rule in King Edward's name. His *former* king ... "I'll bend a knee to him no more ... Set *aside* ..." He pulled the ring from his finger and dropped it beside his untouched meal.

He snatched up the knife beside the plate and thrust it into the now cold slice of mutton. "This!" His hands fisted over his head and the meat wiggled on the blade. Juices from it splashed on his head and ran down his arm. "This life." He shook spray from the meat's liquid on him and gasped for breath. "I gave all in service. In service of my king. I've suffered ..." His breaths came in quick gulps as he glanced around the room. Someone needed to hear. They needed to know. "Suffered ... here ... this bog." No one agreed with him.

He blinked. They'd gone. No one was here. His fists shook in the air, and one still gripped the knife. "All I've endured …" He reached out his hands to the shadows of his men. They surely understood. "I've tried to keep the peace … You know that …. You've fought with me … But these wretches who have no grasp of the concept …" No, no one was there with him. He gripped the knife handle tighter, dropped the mutton on the plate, and pounded blade tip into the plate several more times. "Dismissed …. Set aside … Out of favor …" He moved his panic to the table itself. The tip of the blade sank deep into the dark wood again and again. "'Tis the rain, I tell you. All this water … it prevents me … weighs me down. Released from duty …" His stabs grew rapid and erratic as his word slurred together.

He released a wail of grief and his arms quaked as his fists rose near his face.

He caught his reflection in the honed blade. His face flushed, his stare wild, and his hair unkept. Sintest took one slow, deep breath as silence once more enveloped the room. In that moment, he knew his only option.

"God save the king," he snarled.

He thrust the blade into his chest. It tore through fabric and flesh, but the pain he expected paled in comparison to that caused by the betrayal of the man he given up so much for.

His breaths came in bursts and his knees buckled. Sintest pitched toward the table; his fall sent his meal and dishes crashing to the floor. He soon followed.

"My lord?" his man called through the door.

Sintest's eyes locked onto the last of the visible words of the message smoldering in the hearth; *By order of King Edward.*

Chapter 2

Conwy, Wales

Laden with burdens to carry, the horses snort and shifted their weight between their hooves and made their tack jingle. The mail of forty soldiers rattled with the efforts to prepare for their long journey. Their rumbled conversations added a rich harmony to the growing song. Some hummed with the excitement of a coming adventure. Others, like Angwyn, resented leaving family and home to spread their overlord's power to new lands. But, for Angwyn, accepting the post from issued by the king meant a title again. Edward's missive guaranteed his name and honor would be restored. All that was required was to hold a Scottish keep peacefully in the king's name. The battle for Scotland was said to have been won. Angwyn knew from his own experience, however, that more rebellion was sure to come before the Scots would succumb to a foreign king's rule.

Angwyn glanced down again at the message in his hand. The first words, "By order of King Edward," mocked him. He folded the parchment and stuffed it into his belongings, and resisted the urge to toss it away. He would need it to prove his authority. With a frown, he glared at Castle Conwy gleaming in the bright morning light.

Children's laughter added a sweet melody to the activity's refrain in Angwyn's yard. They scampered around the friar, Brother Gwilim. The cord around the waist of his dark brown robe held a large wooden cross that swayed with his movement. His cowl was pushed back, exposing the warrior's knot he still confined his dark hair in. Gwilim's broad shoulders and honed muscular frame were a contrast to the peaceful robes he wore now. The firm set of his clean-shaved jaw and the hard line of his lips was betrayed by the mirth crinkling the corners of his eyes. "Not today. Not today."

Angwyn didn't believe him any more than the children did. It was a common game they played. The man had no right to play so freely.

One of the soldiers, Hywel, stopped loading the supply wagon. He stomped toward the children waving his hands. "All right. You get, now. Back to your homes."

The children skirted out of the soldier's way but remained close to Brother Gwilim. At thirty-eight, the holy man was only ten years Angwyn's junior, but the man played with the children as though he was one of them. Gwilim winked at the children as he drew a pouch from the folds of his robe.

Angwyn's gaze was drawn from the innocence of youth to the bright heralds adorning men and belongings. They marked each as property of King Edward and his stolen title of Prince of Wales. Angwyn fisted his hands and turned toward his house.

Brother Gwilim passed out the bits of dried fruit to each of the giggling children before they ran off. They passed Angwyn with innocent smiles that made him envious of them.

Angwyn's pounding strides carried him through his home to his bedchamber. Many of his belongings were packed for travel. There was one trunk for Gwendolyn as well. He shifted his gaze to a trunk in the corner. This one would remain. His hand rested on it for a moment and his heart stuttered. He closed his eyes and drew in a deep breath before he eased open the lid.

He laid aside the papers on top without rereading them. Angwyn swallowed hard as he moved the small clothes of a lad he missed more than he could say. He quickly shoved other memories aside in his search as pain sliced through his chest. His fingers brushed something cool and hard. With another deep breath, he secured the item in his hand, and drew it from the bottom of the sorrow-filled container.

Cradling the small sheathed dagger on his palm, Angwyn gazed at the handle adorned with the crest of the true Prince of Wales. With it secure, he hurried to get the contents back out of sight in the trunk.

"Angwyn?"

He dropped the wooden toy he was replacing at the sound of the voice. Gwendolyn stood in the doorway. Her bright smile dimmed as her gaze shifted from his face to the disheveled items of the trunk.

She took a single step into the room. "I …"

Angwyn quickly tucked the dagger in his belt.

Her glance caught the movement and what he tried to hide. Her lips pursed and her eyes filled with tears.

"I ride today for his …"

A tear escaped and slid along her narrow petite nose.

He squared his shoulders. "… for *our* honor."

More tears wet her smooth oval face as she slipped toward him. "It's been twelve years."

Angwyn returned to fumbling with replacing the contents of the trunk. "And yet the pain is real, still, every day. I hear you crying in the night. You cannot deny it."

"No, I cannot. But I do not cry for our son. I cry for you."

Angwyn's hands stilled, and his frantic actions stopped.

Gwendolyn knelt and finished the task of lovingly replacing the items. "You serve the king who took our son. Every day it reminds you. But it cannot be undone."

He stared into her deep brown eyes. "It must be."

"By God's grace alone." She closed the trunk again before she turned to him and offered a small parcel.

Angwyn unfolded the cloth and stared at the dried flower bouquet within.

"When this is done, I pray you return to me again as the man I love."

Angwyn swallowed hard as he nodded and tucked the token of her affection away with the belongings that he would bring. "Our house will know honor once again."

He took her hand and kissed it before he strode from the room. The pounding of his heart almost drowned out the thump of his heels as he crossed though his home again and back into the yard.

Most of the men had completed their preparations. A few nodded as they passed him on the way inside to collect the last of the belongings he'd bring. Forty Welsh men-at-arms stood in relaxed lines. Each were men who rode under his standard and followed his command. This type of honor had come easy once. Swear your allegiance to a good man, fight for his righteous cause, earn honor for your name and your family.

Then came King Edward of England, self-appointed Prince of Wales, a power-hungry tyrant who forced men to bow a knee before him. Angwyn had done it. He'd promised his faithful allegiance, and he, Lord Angwyn Bryn Kenseth born of Conwy in the land of Wales, was a man of his word.

Brother Gwilim stood before the soldiers with his hands in the air. His commanding voice boomed a blessing. "May the Lord answer when you are in distress; may the name of God protect you. May He send you help and grant you support. May He give you the desire of your heart and make all your plans succeed. Some trust in chariots and some in horses, but we trust in the name of the Lord our God."

Angwyn wasn't sure how he felt about asking God to bless their mission to subjugate another nation under Edward's thumb.

Many of his soldiers bent their heads in quiet whispers, ignoring Gwilim's continued holy rally cry.

"All is well?"

Angwyn snapped back from his thoughts, only just then noticing the man beside him.

His captain, Inek Ramonth, fell into step at Angwyn's side. He considered Angwyn for a moment as he waited for reply.

All had to be well. For Gwendolyn's sake, he had to be restored to be the man he once was.

Angwyn noted Gwilim had finished his prayer, at last. "Ready the men, captain. Scotland won't come to us."

Gwendolyn had watched her husband march from their bedchamber, their son's dagger in his belt. In distress, she called to the only One who could help. Her prayer filled the still room. "And he will be a vessel for honorable use, set apart. May it be so, Lord."

She followed in his wake, skirting men coming to retrieve the last of his trunks. Then, she stepped into the morning light. Angwyn and Inek were already mounted. They turned their horses toward the road that would carry them all the way to Scotland.

Angwyn reined in beside her. "I prefer you remain here."

"I can no more refuse him than you can."

"Be on your guard, and be well."

She reached for his hand and he offered it. "And you."

He drew away from her and tapped his horse's flanks with his heels. Two-by-two, the procession passed her with wagons of their supplies mixed among them. She watched until they were out of sight beyond the bend before she allowed her gaze to shift to the Conwy Castle.

Gwendolyn closed her eyes and drew in a deep breath. She released it with a silent prayer. "Be well, my love."

Chapter 3

Scottish Territory

Angwyn had lost count of the days they traveled through the rain. They'd crossed into Scottish territory on their way to Din Osways five days ago. The rolling, emerald Scottish Highlands stretched out around them, but what land wouldn't be vibrant green in the midst of so much rain?

The creak and clatter of the wagons and soldiers behind him stopped. Angwyn turned from the front of their procession winding through the valley to see one of the two wagons in his line mired in the mud.

Gwilim's wagon. The friar clicked his tongue and tapped the reins on the horse's back. "Come on."

Ramonth shouted as he dismounted. Two squires scurried to the back of the wagon. Each youth braced his shoulder against the rear of the wagon and shoved as the horse strained to pull the cart free. One squire lost his footing and slipped to the ground. He rose with one shin caked in thick mud. The young man secured a better grip on the wagon, pressed his shoulder against the wood, and strained. Then, the other youth slipped. The horse churned the mud, digging himself deeper.

Angwyn dismounted. Ramonth stepped to his side.

"What a pig's trough." His captain glanced at his mud-covered boots.

Angwyn snorted. "As if this Scottish mud is somehow worse than that in Wales? It rains in England. It rains in Wales. It rains in Scotland as well."

"But, somehow, the muck in Scotland seems … wetter."

Angwyn understood, but it wouldn't get any better standing here. "Get them moving, captain." He scanned the surrounding hills for danger. As one well acquainted with battle strategy, Angwyn knew the dangers of being stuck in a valley surrounded by high ground. There was excellent cover all around them. The sooner they got moving, the better.

Ramonth stomped toward the wagon. "You there!"

Angwyn considered the muscular man in rough clothing walking on the other side of the well-used road. A Scotsman. The man stopped and glared at Ramonth.

"You," his captain pointed at the burly man. "Free this wagon!"

The squires stopped pushing and the entire procession turned to see what would happen next.

The lone Scotsman looked Ramonth up and down before his gaze flickered to the other soldiers watching him. He released a sharp breath, stomped toward the wagon with a low grumble, and picked up a nearby log.

The squires stepped behind Ramonth.

Saddles creaked and mud slurped as both mounted and foot soldiers shifted their weight.

The Scot stalked forward to stand directly across from Ramonth. The man stood slightly taller than the captain and outweighed Ramonth by at least ten stones.

Ramonth's hand slid to his sword and his palm rested on the pummel.

Only the labored breathing of the horses could be heard as the two men stared at one another.

The Scotsman shoved one end of the log under the wagon and braced the other across his shoulders as he crouched. "Arrgh!"

His roar startled more than just the horse pulling the wagon. Gwilim snapped the reins and the horse lurched forward. When the wagon tore free from the muck, the man rose. Ramonth and the others near the mired vehicle sighed in relief as the wagon dropped safely beside the rut with a soft thud.

With his hard stare still on Ramonth, the Scotsman tossed the log at the captain's feet. Then, he turned and walked away to continue on his journey.

Ramonth turned to the squires with his hand raised to backhand them.

Both lads cowered from the blow that never came.

Angwyn mounted and rode past the three. "That was effective."

Ramonth kept his glare trained on the squires until they ran off, and then stepped out of the way as the procession continued.

Angwyn caught a glimpse of the Scotsman again. He stood on the peak of a small rise to his left. He watched Angwyn's men for a few moments before he spit on the ground, turned his back, and disappeared over the rise to the next hill.

Gwilim's wagon drew alongside him. "Apologies, for the delay."

Angwyn never took his eyes off the road ahead. "You can't help what you can't control."

"Yes ..."

They had barely started moving again when a rider lumbered toward Angwyn and his men. Beside him, Ramonth drew his sword but let it rest in his lap. The wagons and men slowed and the three other mounted soldiers moved to the front.

The rider ambled. He was an English regular, and his surcoat marked him one of Sintest's men. It was stained and hung askew. His light hair was disheveled and unkept.

"Hold, rider," Angwyn shouted. "You are of Din Osways, correct?"

The man drew his horse to a stop before them. "Aye. Who might you be?"

The man must have been away from England for some time to not recognize the crest of a lord. "I am Angwyn Kenseth. By order of the king, I am to replace your lord at Din Osways."

"If you can prove that, I have news."

Angwyn suppressed his fury at being challenged by the lowly guard, but drew his orders and showed them to the man.

The rider stepped his horse forward and leaned to read the parchment. "Well, that explains a few things." He sat back in his saddle. "Sintest is dead."

Angwyn glanced at Ramonth.

"Took his own life after getting a message from the king," the soldier continued. "We figured his wife had gone ill. Must've pushed him over. No great loss, if you ask me. But how is it that you are already here when I am just now taking the message of his death to the king?"

Angwyn just stared. They must have sent this unkempt lout on this errand just to get rid of him.

Realization crossed the soldier's face. "You didn't know he was dead."

"Take your message to the king." Angwyn glanced over the soldier once more. "He resides in Conwy this day." Angwyn kicked his horse forward and the procession began again as the soldier watched them pass.

Ramonth shrugged as his gaze met Angwyn's. "Well, that will make your taking charge a fair sight easier."

As his soldiers followed and the cadence of their steps joined the rattle of mail, and the creak of the wagons, he glanced at the road stretching out before him. What could drive a man to do such an unthinkable action? He drew in a deep breath and released it slowly.

"Do you think he'll make it all the way to the king?" Ramonth snorted.

"If that man has any sense at all, he will."

"Let's hope the king doesn't return him."

Angwyn had the same sentiment.

The rain finally stopped. They had made good progress at its lack. Their path crossed with a group of Scottish women and children who scurried to get out of the way of Angwyn and his men. One lad stopped beside a woman and looked up at him. Angwyn's thoughts were lost as they drifted to another youth on another day…

The battle for Dolwyddelan Castle raged before him. Angwyn sat astride his horse with Ramonth at his side, like always. The air was heavy with the scent of gore and death. War cries and the clash of metal against metal came from every direction as the Welsh soldiers defended their land against the English regulars.

Across the field near the castle wall, the English had surrounded a stand of Welsh squires and pages. Not one lad over the age of seventeen. Only one tall soldier was left to defend the boys. Angwyn and Ramonth were too far away to intercede— but not far enough to avoid seeing the desperate struggle.

Gwilim, flailed wildly at the approaching English. The boys were pressed against the castle wall. There was no direction for escape.

One lad drew a dagger. As Gwilim slashed his sword to the left, the boy struck to the right. The captain spun in time to see the boy pierced through the heart with an English blade. The lad dropped, and the dagger tumbled from his limp hand. Gwilim fell to his knees beside the boy.

Angwyn blinked the Scottish green hills back into focus. His heart hammered as his fingers brushed over that same dagger now in his belt. He again marveled at how his chest could swell with pride, while he shook with rage, as his heart shattered in despair all in the same moment.

Ramonth cleared his throat. "My lord?"

The Scottish lad came back into focus as Angwyn blinked the horrid memory away. While he had stopped and stared at the woman and the boy, the procession of his soldiers had continued.

Ramonth placed a hand on Angwyn's shoulder. Angwyn nodded, turned his mount, and took up a place beside Gwilim's wagon. Ramonth followed as they rode down the road.

The friar paused and Angwyn waited. "… my lord."

"I'm sure one day I will understand why my wife insisted that I bring you along. Tell me, friar, what do you think awaits us in Din Osways?"

"One cannot really know, my lord."

"From what I hear, it can't be much worse than this. They don't seem to fear much of anything other than God. In that, you may have some use after all. Otherwise, let us all hope you are a better cook than you are a savior." Angwyn prodded his horse ahead of the wagon and the friar.

"Yes, my lord." Brother Gwilim crossed himself.

Ramonth called over his shoulder as he passed the wagon himself. "Careful there, friar. Let's not forget which lord we serve."

Angwyn gained on the front of the line at the crest of a small rise. Before him lay a village of less than a hundred structures. A three-towered fortification cast a shadow on them. From the description in his orders from the king, this was Din Osways. The haphazardly arranged village lay between him and the fortification.

As they stared at what some actually dared to call a 'keep,' Ramonth spoke in Welsh. "For the bold, there will be spoils of paradise." He continued in English. "What a dung heap."

"Aye. But it is our dung heap."

Ramonth picked a dirt clod off Angwyn's coat. "But a dung heap it is."

Angwyn only nodded. There were two large forward towers, and one smaller on the south side. But they weren't set evenly around the structure to form the corners. It had a rather unusual shape. The fortifications footprint followed the rocky outcrop on which it set, which may have accounted for the layout. There was a moat with a long bridge stretched out over it. Tendrils of smoke rose from each tower and a few places in the center. "It will do."

Chapter 4

Conwy, Wales

Gwendolyn slid her hand over the fine weave of her linen blue kirtle while Katlyn, who now served as her maid, prepared the warm yellow surcoat for her. As the outer garment was slipped over her head, the color reminded Gwendolyn of a clear spring day, especially when she wore it over the bright blue kirtle. The sleeveless surcoat was only stitch closed from below the collar to her hips allowing the blue skirt of the kirtle to show.

Gwendolyn stood still, as Katlyn tightened the laces down the sides. The soft layers of fabric soon contoured to her womanly figure. Even at her age, Angwyn worried at the way men admired her. But she loved her husband deeply. She drew in a deep breath at his absence. "Lord, watch over him and his men," she whispered as Katlyn left her side and pushed open the shutters over the window.

A breeze off the Conwy River along with warm light from the end of a clear day flooded the room. Light sparkled off the polished wood of the bed, in the gold threads of the tapestries and bedcovers, and off the glass of the mirror. No expense had been spared to adorn these guest chambers.

Gwendolyn slip down onto the small wooden stool. She picked up the light tan boxwood comb from among the items provided to her and ran her finger over the carving. Deer and rabbits stood between two trees that covered the center of the comb. She handed it to her maid who slid the many tines through her long hair.

Once her hair was braided, Gwendolyn held the headband and wimple in place as Katlyn prepared to cover and secure them with the chin strap. Gwendolyn again marveled at the white silk wimple. She rubbed the soft fabric between her fingers. It was going to be hard not to touch it all day.

Knock, knock.

Both women turned toward the door before the headdress was secured. Gwendolyn nodded and Katlyn crossed the chamber and drew the door open.

A squire in hose and a belted tunic that reached his shins nodded to Katlyn. His red and white garments told her that he served the king. He held an ornate box open. "A gift from His Majesty for the Lady Kenseth."

Katlyn considered the contents which looked to be a selection of necklaces and other priceless jewels. The maid removed one necklace.

The squire acknowledged her choice with a nod as he closed the box and turned from the door.

Katlyn draped the long gold chain around Gwendolyn's neck. The pendant was a square of gold. In the center was a round, opaque, dark blue stone. Five pearls dangled from the bottom of the pendant. Gwendolyn brushed her fingers over the piece.

Katlyn secured the wimple and chin strap and Gwendolyn stood to admire her reflection in the tall mirror standing in the corner.

Properly adorned in high English fashion, Gwendolyn stopped at the door and considered her appearance again.

"I can send your regrets, my lady, if you prefer."

"'My lady,' I do enjoy the sound of that."

"It is a pleasure to say, my lady," Katlyn said with a bright grin and a curtsy.

Gwendolyn smiled. "His majesty has been so generous. I would not want him to think me ungrateful."

"Yes, my lady." Katlyn curtsied again and turned to her work of straightening the chamber.

Gwendolyn wound down the stairs of the kitchen tower and out into the late afternoon sun. She crossed the outer ward, stepped up the few covered stairs on the opposite side, and approached the doors to the king's great hall.

Guards, wearing the three-golden-lions crest of King Edward, snapped to attention.

Gwendolyn paused and sighed. "I suppose I will have to get used to that." She smoothed her dress and nodded to the guards, who opened the doors.

Lords and ladies milled about in conversation as others moved to take their places at the long trestle table. High backed chairs painted red lined both sides of the table.

Gwendolyn knew her place. She may have been dressed in noble finery, but she was Welsh. She held her chin high, but not proud; her shoulders square, but not defiant. Not once did she waver as she made her way past the king, at the center of the table, and all the other English nobility to the far end. As she sat, she noted that King Edward had followed her movement. He leaned over and spoke to the man a seat away which made the nobleman between them draw back to stay out of the way.

Edward caught the movement of the flowing yellow garment as the newcomer entered his hall. She was a handsome woman, probably in her late thirties or early forties. A far cry from the teenage girl that scheming king of France, Philip III, had offered as a replacement for her older sister who he'd originally been promised.

Edward pushed his conflict with the French out of his mind as he watched the woman pass and continue to the end of the table. He leaned past Lord Roger Bigod, to his left, to speak with his chancellor on the man's other side. "Tell me Amersham, who is the new guest?"

Walter Amersham looked up from his plate and followed the king's gaze to the lady dressed in bright yellow over rich blue. His chancellor turned back to him with a sly smirk. "That would be Lady Gwendolyn Kenseth, Your Majesty. You invited her to reside in the castle while her husband is up north."

Edward returned the knowing look. "How thoughtful of me."

"I believe she wears a necklace you offered her this evening."

Edward's smile dimmed as he raised a brow to his man. "I offered?"

Amersham nodded as he selected an item from his plate, but didn't put it in his mouth just yet. "Yes, Your Majesty."

"That was generous," Edward grumbled as he straightened in his chair.

Amersham winked. "A well-placed investment, Your Majesty."

Edward considered the man's words, and intentions, for bringing the lovely wife of a Welsh landholder into his castle. She could prove to be a delightful diversion or a great asset. Either way, her presence would be for naught since she sat at the end of the table.

Edward waved a servant close and spoke to him quietly.

Chapter 5

Conwy, Wales

Gwendolyn sat in silence as the English nobility chatted amongst themselves and took no notice of her presence.

"Pardon, my lady." A servant stood at her side. "His Majesty requests that you join him."

A hush fell over those nearest her and Gwendolyn pressed her hand to her collar. "Me?"

The servant reached for the back of her chair to draw it from the table. "Yes, my lady."

She glanced at those staring at her, but nodded to the servant and stood. She followed the servant back toward the king. The rest of the people dining at the king's table stilled as she passed. A strained hush fell over the once lively hall. All eyes were on her.

When she arrived at the king's side, she noted all the seats were occupied. The servant must have been mistaken. Or perhaps someone was playing a cruel joke on the Welsh outsider.

The rest of the room held their breath with her.

Swallowing her fear, she curtsied to the king and waited for whatever fate would befall her next.

King Edward wore a long red tunic covered in an open surcoat of blue trimmed in a wide band of gold. His light curly hair hung to his ears and framed his long face.

The servant cleared his throat and drew the attention of the lord sitting to the king's left. The man looked up and noted her presence. After a glance to the king who held him in a hard stare, the lord rose, and waved at the chair he'd just vacated. "My lady." He turned and left before she claimed his honored seat.

As she lowered into the chair, the servant removed the plate of half-eaten food from in front of her.

Edward considered her with a long gaze. He was even a tall man when he sat, and she had to tip her head to see him clearly. "Such a lovely land you Welsh have, Lady Kensit."

Gwendolyn tried to control her rattling nerves. "It is Kenseth, Your Majesty, and thank you."

The man on her left, who Gwendolyn had seen the king speaking to, stopped. A hunk of peafowl dangled in his fingers as his mouth gaped open.

"Kenseth." Edward drew her hand into his. "I shall have to remember that."

The man on her left returned to his food with a smile.

"Yes, a beautiful land." The king's words were quiet and made Gwendolyn's insides shudder. Still holding her hand, he reached out his other. His fingertips brushed over the top of her dress as he cradled in his palm the pendant she wore. "And a beautiful choice for such a beautiful—" his gaze rose to meet hers—"occasion."

She swallowed and steadied her voice. "Thank you, Your Majesty."

He continued to stare and hold her hand. It might not have ended had the servant not returned with a fresh plate and placed it before her. At last, he released her and returned his attention to his meal.

Gwendolyn fought to slow her pounding heart. Her eyes took a moment to focus on her plate. Sliced apples, peafowl, lettuce, a small egg pie, a fritter, and a slender wedge of aged yellow cheese.

"It is yours."

Gwendolyn startled, and her mind took a moment to connect the king's words. She touched the pendant with the tips of her fingers. "Oh, Your Majesty, I couldn't—"

"No. I will not hear of it."

The weight of her indebtedness to this powerful man settled heavy on her shoulders. "Again, thank you, Your Majesty." The king of England did nothing out of kindness. He was up to something.

They both turned their attention to their meals. Gwendolyn tried to savor the pleasant flavors of the lavish dishes, but her mind tumbled with worry.

"You know," Edward looked to her again. "I will be traveling the land holdings tomorrow. It would be a great pleasure if you were able to join me."

Her heart reignited its furious pace as she paused mid bite and swallowed hard. "Thank you, Your Majesty. That would be lovely."

Edward smiled.

Her mind whirled. The man must know she was married. "My husband shall be pleased to know you take such a personal interest in our land." That should make her situation clear. Though, when he drew back with high-arched brows, she had to reconsider what she'd said. Her breath caught. She'd referred to Wales as their land, not the king's.

He offered a curt nod. "Well yes, of course. Wales is a wonderful addition to the realm. And Scotland as well. There shall be no end to *our* domain."

Gwendolyn pressed forward with a smile. "Yes, Your Majesty. A truly magnificent feat. Will the French be joining us soon as well?" She slipped a slice of apple in her mouth and waited to see if the king's notorious temper would present itself.

Chapter 6

Din Osways, Scotland

Angwyn took in the fortifications as they drew near Din Osways.

The villagers noted their arrival, stopping whatever they were doing to mark the new lord's approach. Moving from the main lane, they formed a long line on either side of the advancing procession.

Angwyn shifted in his saddle. They were eerily quiet. He hadn't expected them to cheer and celebrate their arrival, or even wave. But their still silence gave him pause.

Light and even skin bled through the fabric of the villagers' simple garments. Smudged faces and dirty hands proved they were working people. But their listing homes and sagging roofs proved they had little to show for all their labors.

A lad, not old enough to be a squire, stood by his mother. The boy's eyes widened when he spotted Gwilim. The boy started to make the sign of the cross, but his mother seized his hand and held it tight. Her gaze flicked up and down the line of men to see who might have noticed.

Angwyn again turned his attention to the keep. With the state of the village and its inhabitants, he assumed the wealth would show in the stronghold the English regulars controlled.

The walls were splotched with lichen and moss. Chunks of mortar were missing from many places. The roofs of the three towers looked little better than the village homes. The wooden ramp that led to the first-floor entrance over the dry moat groaned ominously as they crossed. The moat might be the only thing to save them should they ever fall under siege if it wasn't a soggy mud pit drained of its water long ago, or possibly never filled. The walls certainly didn't look up to the task.

Inside the small courtyard, Angwyn did not find things much better. Here, it wasn't villagers, but English regulars, men of Lord Sintest, who lined their way. Dirty torn surcoats hung over their chest. Boots hadn't seen a polish, nor beards a good trim in far too long. No one saluted but they stood slack-armed and watched them enter.

The men were not the only thing lacking. A wooden structure, that no doubt served as a great hall, administrative offices, and living quarters, sat on the north side. Even from the ground, missing shingles could be noticed. Paint of an unknown color peeled from the sides.

Angwyn reined in, swung his leg over his horse, and planted his foot. Muck squished out around the sole of his boot. He noted the ground littered with animal droppings and divots full of water.

Ramonth took more care as he followed his lord out of the saddle. "Secure the horses, unload the wagons, and wait for further instructions," Ramonth told the soldiers and guards as he fell into step beside Angwyn.

Two of his soldiers followed as Angwyn crossed the yard and entered the wooden structure. He removed his gloves, and slapped them into his hand as he noted the cobwebs adorning the corners. The reeds on the floor were caked with mud and green with mold. He added each to the growing list of items he wanted addressed as soon as possible.

As he crossed to what looked like it could have been a meeting room, Angwyn noticed a regular about his age. The Englishman stood behind a woman who was on her hands and knees scrubbing the floor.

This place was going to take a lot of work.

Angwyn stomped into the room, startling the Englishman, who'd been trying to lift the woman's skirt with the end of his pike. He returned weapon handle to the floor and stood at lax attention.

Angwyn cleared his throat and eyed the guard before returning his attention to his captain. "I want a full report as soon as possible. Strengths, strategies, inventories, storehouse, everything."

Ramonth gave him a quick nod. "Yes, my lord."

Angwyn rounded the table and almost tripped over the woman who was still scrubbing the floor. Any woman with any sense would have vacated a room where men were conducting business. But she attended to a large dark splotch on the floor. As she rinsed her rag out in the bucket beside her, he noted two things: none of the stain was removed from the stones, and she was much younger than he thought.

Gwilim stomped into the room with huffed breaths, distracting Angwyn from the young girl who was probably only in her mid-teens.

"And I want to see Sintest's captain immediately."

"Yes, my lord," Ramonth said again.

Angwyn turned to pace and almost stepped on the maid's hand. "Girl, do you need to do that right now?"

She clamored to her feet; the rag tight between her hands. As she stared at the floor, she backed from him with her shoulders hunched tightly.

"You there," Angwyn pointed to the Englishman who had been in the room with her, "take this … girl. Have her clean elsewhere."

The man's eyes swept over the woman who shuddered at his grin. He nodded his agreement.

Gwilim stepped between the Englishman and the maid. "I will take her."

Angwyn glanced between the leering man and the frightened young woman. He turned his gaze to the friar. "Very well. Just do it quickly."

Angwyn didn't miss the hate-filled glare that the regular shot at the friar and the departing girl. He turned toward the soldiers who had followed him, and the remaining guard. "The rest of you, out as well. The captain and I have much to discuss."

The room emptied of all but Ramonth. Angwyn threw his gloves on the table. His captain laughed as he dropped into a chair.

Angwyn saw nothing humorous in their present situation. His gaze caught on fresh scratches and deep punctures on the table near where his gloves had landed. He ran his finger over them.

"You must admit, Lord Sintest was not well." Ramonth said with a lingering chuckle.

"To lose the favor of the king is never well. Still, a sane man doesn't plunge a blade into his own heart. But what is Edward's play in all this?"

Ramonth drummed his fingers on the table. "Sintest was a failure. The rebels run rampant across his lands. Add to that you are well respected in Wales."

Angwyn turned his attention to his captain. "Therefore, either an ally or a threat."

"What better way to ensure your loyalty than to send you far away under the guise of giving you everything you've ever wanted?" Ramonth shrugged and settled back in his chair.

Angwyn clasped his hands behind his back. Ramonth saw the truth of the matter so clearly. "It seemed such a simple choice when the offer was made." And it had. Too simple, now that he thought about it.

"It seems to me the right choice was made." His captain glanced around the room and Angwyn followed his gaze. Of all they had seen so far, this room was appointed with several fine chairs and a tapestry on the wall. Other than the stain on the floor, it was clean and well maintained. "Not bad for two kids from Gyffin," Ramonth said with a grin.

Angwyn sighed. "Maybe so." He turned and glanced out the window.

"Settle in the men, captain. It has been a long journey."

"Yes, my lord." Ramonth pushed to his feet and headed for the door.

"Inek?"

"Yes?"

"It has been a long time since I was called 'lord' by anyone who mattered."

"If I have my way, that honor will never be removed from you again."

Angwyn continued to stare out the window as he nodded. The sound of his captain's firm footfalls over the stone floor faded. Still, that title would come at a price.

Chapter 7

Din Osways, Scotland

Angwyn's gaze swept over the meeting chamber and fell on the stain. The near black blob had to be Sintest's blood. Why had no one thought to clean it before now?

Nothing about this ill-maintained keep would change with him standing here alone. With a huff, he stomped out of the room. He followed Gwilim's voice into the larger room that served as the great hall —though calling it great was beyond ridiculous.

"Now, you will be safe in here," Gwilim said to the young maid who stared at the floor beside the friar at the other end of the room. "My name is Gwilim."

The maid nodded. "Isabelle," she said.

Gwilim stood with his shoulders square as though he stood at attention and barked orders to the men he trained. "You can teach me about this land while you help me in the kitchen. Are you hungry?"

The maid glanced up at Gwilim.

"I saw apples …" Gwilim's words were halted as he turned and noted the two guards who entered the hall.

Angwyn paused in the shadow of the hallway to the meeting room to see what would happen. He needed to learn what manner of men he had just inherited under his command. Although, he didn't hold out much hope after meeting the guard on the road.

Gwilim gave them the quick appraising look. "I will have the meal ready in a couple of hours."

"That's not why we're here," said the taller man with long, unkept hair. He'd been the regular in the meeting chamber.

Both Gwilim and Angwyn watched the way the Englishmen's stare swept over the maid. Angwyn's hands fisted, and his skin heated. He did not care for any of the behavior he saw from the English dogs. They were not proper soldiers.

Gwilim offered them an innocent smile. "Oh, my mistake. And what exactly is it that you need? Confession perhaps?"

A lot of it, by Angwyn's estimation.

The two guards glanced at one another and shifted the weight between their feet.

Gwilim's arms extended as he emphasized his booming words as though he preached from the pulpit. "Confession is a blessing for the soul. Such a relief to unburden yourself, is it not?" He didn't wait for them to agree. "Have you said your prayers today?" Again, Gwilim didn't pause. "You mustn't start your day without your prayers. How else do you expect the Lord Almighty to show you His favor. You haven't, have you?" He took only a breath to look directly at each man.

"Well, let us start with that." Gwilim waved his arms at them as though they were scattered chickens he was trying to get back in the coup. He shooed them toward the door they entered. "Yes, now. You two go say your prayers and we can speak later about the rest."

Gwilim's imposing, muscled presence forced the men to back toward the door.

"And I do expect you to bathe before I feed you a meal," the friar said with a smirk as he crossed his arms.

The maid offered the commanding holy man a slim smile as Gwilim returned to her side.

"I think it best that we send you home while things settle. There will be plenty we can talk about tomorrow. Don't you think?"

The maid nodded.

The friar crossed himself. "Gu'n deanadh Dia thu. Did I say that right?"

The maid gave a small shake of her head. "May God be with you, Gum biodh Dia maille riut," she said softly as she strolled toward the door.

The friar watched her go before his gaze swung toward Angwyn, now standing fully in the hall. "I wonder what it was I did say?"

Conway, Wales

Gwendolyn slipped into her chambers with a sigh.

Katlyn looked up from her sewing, set it aside quickly, rose, and dipped in a curtsy. "My lady, my apologies. You are back early."

"I am afraid that you were right in your worries. The duties of court are far too exhausting." All those clamoring for favor with the king; the nuance of determining who to shun and who to favor to raise your status; and the sudden change in those tides would make any head spin.

Once the meal had concluded, all the ladies who'd refused to acknowledge her when she'd first entered, had gathered around and wanted to know all about her. Their constant chatter and viscous gossip had hurt Gwendolyn's ears.

Katlyn moved beside her and pulled at the ties under her right arm on the surcoat to loosen them.

Gwendolyn's smiled. "However, his majesty is quite charming." She'd heard of his temper and been surprised at his kindness.

"Yes, my lady."

Gwendolyn's gaze slid to her reflection in the mirror.

Katlyn paused and their gazes met in the glass. "You will be with Lord Kenseth again soon."

"Yes, but when will Lord Kenseth again be with me?" she muttered. She'd spoken true when she'd told Angwyn that she prayed he'd return to her as the man she loved.

Katlyn's hand rested on her arm. Such a sweet gesture and probably something that would have been frowned upon by those English ladies of court. But it touched Gwendolyn's heart. She placed her hand over the maid's with a smile. She gave the girl's hand a couple of pats before Katlyn retuned her attention to loosen the ties at her side. "I pray daily that he finds what he seeks."

Gwendolyn's gaze turned to look out the window at the stars. "It's been twelve years."

Kaylyn's hand stilled for a moment as though she might have offered up a quick prayer as well. Soon, she was back at work loosening the surcoat.

Angwyn weighed heavy on Gwendolyn's mind. "Do you believe he is at rest?"

Katlyn moved to her left side to work on the laces there. "Young William is with our God in heaven, my lady. There is no greater rest than that."

Gwendolyn's arm lowered, preventing the maid from continuing. Her other hand she held over her mouth, fighting back tears. She looked at the young woman.

"My lady. I am sorry." Katlyn nipped at her fingertips.

"It is fine, child. I will finish from here."

Katlyn bowed her head. "My lady."

Gwendolyn turned and smiled. "It is fine."

The maid curtsied, gathered her things in haste, and scurried from the room.

Gwendolyn took a few steps toward the window. The breeze of the Conwy River soothed her. "Dear Lord, protect my love. I cannot stand to lose him too."

Chapter 8

Din Osways, Scotland

Angwyn stood atop the curtain wall of the fortification he spent weeks to reach. He held the Scottish keep in the name of King Edward of England. The English regulars who had served as Sintest's guards joined his own soldiers in the dining hall below. Their revelry floated up to him. He wished he could share in it.

Part of him wanted to participate in the joy of a journey finally ended. But Angwyn served a king he hated. A man who had extended his lands through war—a war that had taken the life of Angwyn's young son. William had only been thirteen when an English regular ran him through. For all Angwyn knew, that very man could be in the hall bellow, drinking merrily with his men.

Ramonth stumbled from the hall into the courtyard below. He held a mug in his hand as he swayed through the dim light. As he passed two guards, he raised his mug in salute. They responded in kind.

Angwyn sighed. "Not bad for two kids from Gyffin." He repeated the captain's words from earlier. He should be proud to be called on by the king to hold this land. But it all sat ill on his soul.

He moved to the nearest tower and up a short flight of stairs to the room that would serve as his chambers while he held this keep. Lord Sintest's belonging were piled in the corner and his own trunks stacked around the room. It would take a day or two to get his belongings sorted and the room functional.

He reached into his vest and withdrew the dried flowers Gwendolyn had gifted him. Gently, he sat them on a small table near the bed in a place of honor where he would see them often. He wanted to be the man she needed again. A man of true honor, not nobility gifted to him by a man he didn't respect as a way to keep him in line.

He turned from the token of his wife's affection and stared through the window at the fire lights glowing from the village. These people had more in common with his own than he did with the English. They were being forced under Edward's thumb, like Wales had been. And now, he was a part of their subjugation.

He pulled a bound set of parchments from the stack of Sintest's belongings and settled into a comfortable chair. He rested his feet on top of a trunk and opened the report the previous lord recorded of his time in Din Osways. It started out as any military report; the number and names of the men who had come with him, the state of the keep and the village when he arrived, the store and supplies. Sintest had started out just like Angwyn was now.

How long before he also slipped into madness?

Ramonth climbed the stairs behind a squire carrying a breakfast tray. Even if the lad hadn't been entering the lord's chamber and wearing his colors, Ramonth would have known the lad was a Welsh squire. He was clean and in good order. A lean youth, maybe a year away from his spurs, and he already took his duty seriously.

The large lord's chamber would have been spacious, taking up the whole top floor of the tower, if not for all the trunks stacked around.

Inside, the squire pulled up short and Ramonth almost bumped into him.

Sunlight flooded the room and covered Kenseth, who was asleep in a chair. His boot-covered feet were propped up on a trunk. After all the nights on the journey sleeping on a bedroll, Ramonth had enjoyed a bed. His friend looked to have gotten lost in a tome that now teetered on his lap.

Ramonth smirked and leaned over the squire. He pulled the tray from his hands and whispered. "I'll take that."

The squire bowed respectfully and slipped from the room. The smart lad had the good since to ease the chamber door silently closed behind him.

Ramonth turned to the table at one end of the chamber and moved the plates from the tray to the polished wood surface. He popped a slice of pork in his mouth, and spread butter on a piece of bread, which followed the pork. It was good to be a soldier of rank and title in the king's army. They were men of honor and respect now, and the position afforded the outcast Welsh men the best Edward had to offer.

Ramonth turned and quickly scanned of the room. He was alone with Kenseth. He moved across the room on the balls of his feet and slid behind the sleeping lord. The metal serving tray still in one hand, Ramonth drew his dagger from his side as he neared the lord of the keep. He had known the man most of his life, and he knew exactly where they were going from here. Only upward.

When he stood directly behind the man, Ramonth raised his dagger. He took a little wider stance and reached the dagger closer to the side of the lord's head. Unable to control the grin playing on his lips every muscle rippled in excitement. He twisted the dagger in his hand and slammed the handle into the metal tray.

Clang!

Kenseth shot to his feet sending the bound parchments to the floor. He whirled toward the threat and his sword drew half way from its sheath. His wide gaze locked on Ramonth and narrowed quickly as his featured hardened.

"Good morning, my lord," Ramonth said with a bright smile.

Kenseth scowled and thrust his sword fully into the sheath. "One day, Inek, I will gut you." He rubbed his hands over his face and bent to retrieve the parchments.

Ramonth strolled back toward the table. "I hate being called Inek, and you know you're not quick enough for that." He placed another slice of pork in his mouth and chewed a moment. "Never have been. That's why you need me. Shall I gather the men?"

Kenseth turned the chair he'd slept in toward the table and plopped it down with a bang before he sat. He took a couple of bites before he nodded.

Chapter 9

Din Osways, Scotland

Angwyn stood on a low platform overlooking the keep's courtyard with his hands clasped behind his back. Ramonth watched at his side, arms cross and feet apart. In the few hours that his men had been here, the courtyard had been cleared of its muck, the surface leveled, refuge removed, and supplies put away in an orderly fashion. It released some of the tension Angwyn had been holding since he laid eyes on the ill-kept mess.

Sintest's guards were still another matter. Few had bothered to clean or don better garments—perhaps they had none remaining. Each of the former lord's men sparred with one of his soldiers. The clack of their staves echoed off the surrounding defensive walls. Their battle skills looked as deplorable as the rest of their condition.

One of the guards the friar who had encountered in the hall as he watched over Isabelle sparred nearby. The guard foolishly eyed Gwilim as he passed. Taking advantage of the distraction, Angwyn's soldier, Eudav, swept the guard's legs out from beneath him, and the guard landed hard on his back with a grunt.

"Not horrible," Angwyn muttered.

His captain didn't agree. "They'll do fine keeping the villagers in line. But what if Edward calls on us to fight?"

"His Majesty has his own forces."

Another pair drew Angwyn's attention. Hywel sparred with a guard almost a head taller and considerably heavier than him. Hywel moved with the honed precision of his training and clocked the guard upside the head. The guard dropped unconscious at Hywel's feet.

Ramonth snorted. "Let us hope so."

Kenseth squared his shoulders. There was work to be done. "Line them up, captain."

Ramonth snapped to attention. "Yes, my lord."

Angwyn drew his riding gloves from his belt and descended the platform.

Ramonth pointed to Hywel. "Well? Wake him up."

The soldier dropped his stave as Angwyn passed him. Hywel grabbed the bucket of water they'd all been using to drink from, and splashed the contents on the guard's face.

The man jerked away with a curse and tossed his shaggy head, which sprayed droplets of water in every direction.

Yes, there was indeed a lot of work to be done.

Angwyn settled in his saddle as he left the keep down the creaky gangway. He released a deep breath when his horse's hooves thumped across the hard earth. He exchanged a quick glance with Ramonth at his side. Without saying a word, both men agreed; fortifying the wooden bridge was first on their lists of projects.

Angwyn turned back to the task at hand and led his men and Sintest's guards into the village. As their procession approached, the villagers stopped what they were doing and turned to watch. Others stepped out from their homes and join their neighbors on the edge of the street.

A lad with red glistening in his wavy hair looked up with a determined set of his jaw. He reminded Angwyn of William. Next to the youth was a woman and a tall burly Scotsman who carried an air of authority in his hefted chin.

"That's a big man," Ramonth said. Angwyn glanced at his captain with a raised brow and Ramonth continued. "We'll have to keep an eye on him."

Angwyn looked back at the high-ranking family and the village he would control. Getting this man to fall into line would be key to his success.

The lad, who looked a little younger than William had been, turned from the woman's side and slipped between two of the buildings. Angwyn wasn't concerned. He doubted the boy would find any interest in the affairs of his elders.

As the procession turned into the narrow lanes, and made their way to the village center, Angwyn caught glimpses of the lad darting behind the huts and marking their progress. Maybe he found something of interest, after all.

Angwyn reined in on one side of the village center. Empty booths marked where the vendors sold their wares on market day. Shop owners emerged from the businesses around the edge of the space. A well sat prominently on one side. He turned and faced the crowd over the heads of his soldiers and guards. The men under his control stood in ranks between him and the villagers.

As the town folks filled the other side of the village center, Angwyn noted their number and condition. There looked to be over two-hundred, families mostly, though, perhaps, fewer men than he expected. That could have been due to a few factors. The men could have been out hunting or tending fields, they could have been killed in skirmishes with Edward's forces, or—by far the worst possibility for Angwyn—the missing men could have been in the countryside with their fellow rebels, preparing the next attack.

He'd worry about that possibility later. Now, as the villagers quieted and it looked like all who were coming had taken up their places, Angwyn straightened in his saddle. He drew in a deep breath and scanned the crowd. A shadow moved at the corner of the nearest building. A smile tugged at Angwyn's lips. The lad would have had a better vantage point next to his big father.

He turned his attention back to those gathered. "People of Din Osways, I am Lord Angwyn Bryn Kenseth of Conwy. I have traveled long to this land and eager to bring the glory of England to this place." Those last words burned his throat.

The sly boy poked his head out a little further.

"By decree of King Edward …" A flash of movement from the lad's direction caught Angwyn's eye. "I am—" A clod of mud splatted against his right temple, slid down Angwyn's cheek, and dripped onto his shoulder.

The boy dashed into the shadows.

Half of his soldiers smashed into guards as they gave chase with angry shouts. The other half tightened their protective ring around him to stave off a more serious attack.

Angwyn wiped the mud away with the sleeve of his forearm as he scanned for any others directing their wrath at him. Some villagers snickered, others nodded their approval, a few gasped and pulled their children close.

The guards lunged at the crowd with their weapons raised. Mothers yanked their children out of their path and tried to run for home. The men stood their ground, blocking any strike with whatever they had at hand; a staff, a rake handle, an eating knife, a pitchfork. The villagers never attacked as they fought off the onslaught of the guards, but they weren't giving ground either.

"Men!" Angwyn's men jerked, ready for his next command. Sintest's guards only intensified their assault of the people. "Guards of—"

A guard near his horse's flank seized a man by the shirt and yanked him forward. The villager wrapped the guard in a fearsome embrace to prevent the guard from swinging his sword. The two crashed into the side of Angwyn's mount.

The startled horse reared and danced to the side, sending his soldiers and nearby villagers scrambling to get out of the way.

Angwyn tugged on the reins and clamped his legs hard against the prancing animal. It gave one final toss of its head and a snort.

Ramonth rode past. "That was effective."

Angwyn sat one hand on his thigh and surveyed the chaos caused by the guards' overreaction to one child's antics. There was so much work to be done. And now his efforts to establish working relations with the Scots under his leadership would need to be doubled.

A guard struck a woman in the head with the hilt of his weapon as she shielded an older boy. Blood dripped from her wound.

Angwyn tightened his hands on his reins. Time to stop the madness.

Chapter 10

Conwy, Wales

Gwendolyn's fingers played with the satin ribbon sewn in silver thread around the edge of her dangling sleeves. The splendor of the dark green kirtle and bright blue surcoat were spoiling her and she couldn't keep the smile from her lips.

The silk wimple brushed her cheek as she exited the tower into the busy ward. Nobility stood about in their own finery, their conversations animated, and their laughter a little too loud. Servants ran from the kitchen and other buildings to the wagons and back. The king's dark, ornately carved carriage waited near the front of the line of other carriages and saddled horses.

Gwendolyn squared her shoulders and slowly strolled toward a group of ladies she had spoken with last night. She played with the necklace the king had gifted her, rubbing it between her thumb and finger.

"Lady Kenseth," a familiar voice called before she reached the group. King Edward was dressed in a long, belted tunic that almost touched his tall boots. Over it, he wore an open red surcoat trimmed in fur. He smiled.

She turned and quickened her pace to meet him.

Edward offered her a small bow. "Good morn to you, my lady."

She curtsied deep. "Good morn, Your Majesty."

A wagon with two high-backed chairs, stacks of folded linens, and crates for metal plates and goblets rolled past them in a cacophony of discordant noise.

Edward followed her gaze and waited for the noise to dim. "They go to prepare a place for our meal."

Another wagon followed the first, which was full of kegs of wine, cooking pots, and bags of fruits.

"It looks as though you have planned for a feast, Your Majesty."

He smiled again with a nod. "It should be a nice treat. I thought we'd go north to the sea for our meal." He asked her about the coastal area not far north of the city as they talked for a short time. Court officials interrupted from time to time to ask after his wishes on one matter or the other for the coming day.

At last, all was ready and he waved out his hand directing her. "I have prepared my carriage for you."

Gwendolyn curtsied again. "Your Majesty, I couldn't—"

He offered his hand. "I will hear no more about it. Come, Lady Kenseth." He led her to the small, two-wheeled coach and helped her step inside. The square wagon had four large openings, one on each side. A curved roof arched above her. The small, enclosed space contained a single padded bench which forced the rider to face backward from the direction they were traveling. Edward handed Katlyn a small stool and motioned her maid to join Gwendolyn inside the carriage.

Edward gathered the reins of his black horse and took the saddle with a flourish of his red surcoat. He spoke to several others before he raised his hand. "Let us be to our adventure." His horse moved through the gate ahead of his carriage. A long string of mounted nobles and others in carriages followed.

"This is very exciting," Katlyn said as she stared out the windows on either side of them.

Gwendolyn settled into the rhythm of the carriage's movement as it wound through the city that Edward had built within the walls next to the castle. The English held their businesses and homes here. The Welsh, if they were allowed to live within the city at all, were servants and labors.

Surrounded by the finery of the crown, the king's favor, and yet knowing it all came at the cost of her people, sat at odds within her.

Edward drew alongside the carriage in the wider streets. "Such a fine summer day, wouldn't you agree, Lady Kenseth?"

"Yes. The good Lord has shown His favor on us."

Edward hummed in agreement as he again moved forward to pass through the city gates.

It was a beautiful day for a ride in such luxury through the Welsh country. Gwendolyn's heartbeat increased, and she sat a little straighter as she took in all their surroundings.

Lord Walter Amersham served as the king's chancellor. A position he'd worked hard to get and retain. Amersham strolled along a pass through the trees with Edward at his side. They'd taken a private meal and now joined the others following their picnic on the shore. The waves lapped gently onto the sand. His plan was progressing at a pleasing rate. He would have his prize sooner than he hoped.

The glen was dotted with lounging English nobility around heavy cloths sprinkled with the last of their meal. Servants dashed about, clearing away the dishes and returning them to the wagons. Some men stood around chatting.

As Amersham and Edward stepped from the more concealed path to the open area of the gathering, he watched a couple pass in front of Lady Kenseth. She sat regally on the queen's chair next to the king's. The royal carriage behind her framed her in nobility she did not possess.

"You have done well, Amersham."

Several men bowed as the king approached. Amersham smiled and kept his comments hushed. "With the lords that have moved north, the lands here do need to be maintained. All in the service to the throne, Your Majesty."

"Of course." Edward surveyed those gathered. They straightened their garments, offered him observance—anything to gain his favor. "We offer them trinkets and they snatch them up like they were precious gems. It is amazing what a man's ego will make him do."

"Well, I …"

"The Welsh, Lord Amersham. The Welsh." He glanced at Gwendolyn again.

Amersham chuckled softly. "Yes, of course. These people are a rather pedestrian lot."

Edward leaned toward Amersham who stood to his left. "Now, surely Amersham, you can't mean all of them."

Amersham smirked. "Present company excepted, of course."

Edward moved to stand before the woman.

As Amersham approached the lady beside the king, Amersham, overheard a bit of her conversation with her maid.

Gwendolyn hadn't noted their arrival yet. "I have to admit, I am rather enjoying this. Even if it is just for the moment."

The maid collected her dishes. "Yes, my lady. I'm sure Lord Kenseth will have an equally noble court prepared for your arrival."

Amersham thought of the lady's troublesome husband. He steeled himself. All in good time. Clearly the simple Welsh girl had no notion of the barbarity of the Scottish lands. Not that he'd be allowing the lady to join her husband. He needed her close to keep both her husband constrained and the king distracted.

Gwendolyn's gaze rose to look out over the wide sea. "It seems so foreign to think of Scotland in such a way as this."

"And what way would that be?" Edward said.

Lady Gwendolyn stood hastily before the king and her maid stopped what she was doing to curtsy.

Edward sat. The stares of the other nobility again took in the place of honor Edward gave to this simple Welsh woman. She smiled sweetly at him.

Edward returned a knowing look before he steeled his expression and turned to Lady Gwendolyn and waved her toward the seat. "Please, sit. I greatly desire to visit a while."

As the lady moved slowly to sit beside him, her gaze rose to all those staring at her. She fidgeted in her seat and sat rigidly.

Edward ignored the gawking and glanced up at the sky. "Tell me, Amersham, do you think it looks like rain?"

Amersham raised his gaze to the bright blue sky that held nary a cloud. "Quite possibly, Your Majesty." He clapped his hands loudly which caused Gwendolyn to startle. "Come now, let's get this cleaned up and packed away. You there— "he pointed to a maid— "see those plates are put back in the crates." He pointed to two male servants. "As soon as a crate is filled, put it back in the wagon." He turned to the nobles. "Come now, people, we don't want to get caught in a downpour."

Everyone glanced at the sky, and then at Edward and Gwendolyn before they, too, directed their personal servants to begin cleaning up.

As the others busied themselves and moved away, Edward turned to Gwendolyn with a smile and Amersham rubbed his hands together. Indeed, his plan was working quite well.

Chapter 11

Din Osways, Scotland

Angwyn swiped rain from his eyes. A roll of thunder bubbled over the hills. His horse tossed his head and additional water splattered from his mane over Angwyn. He huffed a sigh almost as loud as his horse's snort.

"Come on."

"Move along."

His men shoved the last of the citizens of Din Osways into their homes. Hywel's boots slashed through the puddles and he stomped toward Angwyn. "My lord, the village has been cleared as you ordered."

It seemed like the best solution at the time. With the people indoors, no one else would challenge his authority. It also served to separate the cruel guards from the villagers. He huffed again. This day had been fruitless. He only wanted to introduce himself. One innocent boy's prank and chaos had turned him from a benevolent leader, to a tyrant using his men to restore order.

"And the boy?" Perhaps he could restore a little good will between him and the people if they saw him deal fairly in the punishment of the lad.

Hywel squinted against the rain falling in his eyes as he looked up at Angwyn. "Not found, my lord. Shall we punish one of the others?"

Good heavens, even his own men looked to punish the innocent for the minor crimes of a misguided youth. "Punish? What punishment would you suggest?" He raised his arm to the black pouring sky. "Tell me, soldier, which side of this is standing in the rain and which is not?"

He pulled on the reins to move his horse around his man. Hywel glanced at the sky and his sodden garments. He waved at the soldiers with him and they fell into line behind Angwyn.

Movement on a hill caught his eye, but Angwyn couldn't make out anything through the gloom and rain. Perhaps the lad watched him leave like the boy had watched him arrive. Wherever he was, the lad would have to be dealt with—and soon if he was ever to have any kind of authority with these people.

He kicked his horse to speed. Rain dashed his face with a thousand tiny stings. This was not a good start at all.

Warmed by the fire and in dry garments, Angwyn followed the ruckus to the hall. The small space was filled with men. Lord Sintest's guards sat to one side and his soldiers to the other. Few had chosen to view the other as fellow men-at-arms. His men talked and laughed. The guards hoisted their tankards in the air with loud shouts that were answered by others. Ale sloshed out on the table before they downed a hearty draft and thumped it back on the table, only to have another pick his up and start the scene all over again.

He turned to the table that set perpendicular to the others at the front of the room and joined Ramonth. The meal of roasted boar, cheese, hard bread, and cooked apples was enjoyable even as the guards' volume and antics grew the farther they fell into their drink.

Gwilim's dangling cross swayed and the hem of his robe fluttered as he hurried between the tables and brought them food or cleared plates.

Angwyn ate in silence, taking in the scene. The events of the day ran though his thoughts in an unending loop. He failed to see what he could have done differently and struggled to come up with the best way to deal with the lad when he was found.

With a frustrated grunt, he popped the last bite of apple slathered in honey into his mouth and pushed his plate away. Angwyn pinched the bridge of his nose. This day had started out with such promise. Then, one boy had lashed out, the guards had gone after the villagers, and the endless rain drenched them. Now, the drunken frivolity of those same ill-trained men caused the ache in his head to grow into an incessant pounding. He coughed. It would be just his luck to be stricken with a cold after such a disastrous beginning here.

Gandry, the guard who had been in the room with Isabelle when Angwyn arrived, and two other guards he'd yet to learn the names of, left the hall together.

Ramonth was still finishing his meal. "You were right."

"Of course I was." Angwyn glanced at his captain. "What about?"

He had to wait as Ramonth took a bite of sliced of boar that he'd stacked on a slice of bread. He didn't quite finish chewing before he answered. His words were mumbled around his food. "He makes a better cook than a priest." The captain raised his chin toward Gwilim. He finished his bite and wiped his mouth with the back of his hand. "Not that I have had much use for a priest."

Angwyn chuckled. "Much to my wife's annoyance."

"She has never truly approved of me."

"Oh, she approves as far as she believes your lies that you are quicker with the sword. I am also sure she believes she will manage to convert you some day." Angwyn had, in fact, overheard Gwendolyn's prayers for the captain's soul on many occasions.

Gwilim stepped to their table and added Angwyn's empty plate to the stack he carried. Their gazes met for a moment, before the friar ducked his head and hurried to the next table. Angwyn watched him leave.

"The man is doing his job," Ramonth said with a grunt.

Angwyn glanced at his captain. How could the man not understand what it was like to see Gwilim's face every day? To know how he had failed. To remember at every turn what the man had cost him.

Ramonth wiped his mouth again. "Apologies, my lord." He returned his attention to his plate.

Angwyn's gaze again fell on the friar as he marched about with the same military efficiency he had once trained Angwyn's men. "There are some things that just cannot be forgiven."

"They say forgiveness is a blessing to the forgiver, more so than the forgiven."

"Now, *you* sound like my wife."

Ramonth shrugged and took a bite of a honey-covered fruit. "Maybe so. Does that make it less true?" He nodded toward the friar again.

Angwyn watched him. A calm peace graced the man's face and a bounce filled his step—even with his height. Gwilim embodied peace. How was that fair? What right did that man have to be so content?

Ramonth pushed his empty plate away. "God or not, your sour puss would make anyone want to be more like him any day."

Did he care that the men wanted to model themselves after the friar and not him? If he was to be their leader, should he not try harder to be a more placid type of man? But how did he become such a man when his heart still ached?

Ramonth picked up his tankard and brought it toward his mouth. He glanced inside and plopped it back on the table with a thump.

Angwyn smirked. It must have been empty for now his captain had a 'sour puss.'

The guards' volume grew yet again. One shoved another good-naturedly, but when he bumped into the man on the other side of him, shouts were exchanged. Fists rose in the air as men came off their benches.

Angwyn was actually glad for the distraction. "You have your work cut out for you, captain."

Ramonth's head shot up as he straightened. "I?"

"You are now the captain of the guard, are you not? You don't expect me to discipline this lot, do you? This day was not our best display." Angwyn's men had been controlled and followed orders. Sintest had left his men in as poor condition as the keep and the village. It was going to take a lot of work to get these men back in line. His captain was just the person to see to the task.

Ramonth shrugged again. "Let them be. It is just our second night."

Angwyn stood, turned, and leaned over his chair toward his captain. "And when is the right time to raise my expectations? Do not let them forget their place, captain. The only difference between a mercenary and a rogue is the amount of food in his belly. I'll keep them fed. You keep them in line."

Ramonth had the good sense to look chastised. "Yes, my lord."

Angwyn thought Ramonth would raise his tankard for more ale, but he pushed it away as Angwyn stepped from the table and crossed the room to head toward the tower and his chamber.

Chapter 12

Conwy, Wales

Gwendolyn hadn't spoken on the ride home. The afternoon had played again in her head as she relived each moment. From the grandeur of the ride in the royal coach, to the pampered decadence of a fabulous meal that she had no hand in growing, gathering, or preparing, as well as the attention of the king, it had been like a dream.

She all but floated up the stairs to her luxurious chamber. She replayed her long conversation with the king as Katlyn helped her out of her wimple and gowns. He had busied everyone else so they could speak almost privately—though they had never truly been alone. He had all but turned his chair to face her directly as she held him in rapt attention.

Katlyn slid the nightgown over Gwendolyn's head. Even this simple shift was of the finest and softest material. She sighed dreamily as she sat and unwound her braid. Afterward, she drew the silver handled brush in slow long strokes through her hair.

The king had asked her questions about her life as a young woman in Wales. He'd attended to ever word, laughed at her humorous antics of youth, and nodded in understanding at her challenges. He had let her do most of the talking and had only asked questions now and then.

Occasionally, he'd shared a similar story from his youth. "Was the day not wonderful?"

Katlyn paused from putting her clothes away. "My lady?"

She sighed again. How long had it been since she had been treated like a person who mattered? When was the last time a man treated her with such deference and attention? She felt like she was being courted again. "It has been so long. I was afraid I had forgotten." In fact, she hadn't even realized how much she had missed the care and connection.

"You handled yourself magnificently, my lady. His majesty seemed quite amused."

As was the case previously, her maid had misunderstood. She hadn't been talking about her comportment with those at court. She'd referred to being treated like a person who mattered. But she smiled at how many times King Edward had chuckled at her tales. "Yes, he did."

Katlyn turned down her bed. "Shall we send a letter to Lord Kenseth?"

The brush held still as the thought of her distant husband—both in his placement in Scotland, and in his attention of her. "Tomorrow," she mumbled as she let her husband fade and the memory of King Edward return.

Din Osways, Scotland

Angwyn coughed again as he strolled toward his chamber. "Damn Scottish rain." Dealing with the villagers as he became soaked on his horse today had done him no service.

As he rounded the corner at the top of the stairs, he found a group gathered near his door. Gandry and the two guards who seemed to travel everywhere with him stood in front of a line of four girls. Their attire and appearance spoke of them being from the village. The young women stood with their backs pressed against the wall, arms crossed tight or hands clasped before them so their skin turned white, and their heads were bowed low. While the men muttered between them, the girls were silent.

"What is this?" Kenseth had had enough today. He could think of no good reason for the group to be outside his door.

"A celebration, m' lord." Gandry swayed slightly as he hoisted his fist in the air. "A celebration of today's victory." The other two men failed to contain their snickers, as Gandry winked, and attempted to bring his wayward finger to his lips but failed to hold it there as he tried to silence them.

"You are drunk." Angwyn's words growled.

The men only straightened as if they stood under inspection. "Yes, m'lord." Gandry said with too much pride in the feat.

"Be gone. All of you." He would need to be clearer with his captain. This behavior was unacceptable of men under his command.

"M' lord, 'tis tradition that the lord of the keep be able to choose his —" He hiccupped, or paused to cover his words. "—his own … chambermaid. As you have just arrived, we thought it good that you might choose tonight."

"I need no chambermaid." He had been without one since Wales had fallen, along with his standing as a nobleman.

Gandry's lopsided drunken smirk annoyed him. "Oh, but, m'lord, you wouldn't want to break tradition. After all, everyone needs a bit of a chambermaid every now and then." The man attempted to wink again, and he drew Angwyn's attention back to the silent girls.

Angwyn considered the young women who were probably all in their late teens. Would it be another afront to the villagers if he denied one of their daughters the honor of working for the lord in the keep? Here, she would have access to better food and living accommodations in one of the servant's quarters.

"Tradition, m'lord," Gandry whispered loudly again.

While it might have been best to select one, he was tired. It could be handled at another time. "It is late. Go to your quarters."

Gandry's swaying arm drew his attention back to the girls again.

Angwyn huffed. "If I choose, you will end this and depart?"

"Oh, yes, m'lord." Gandry nodded vigorously, which made his unkept hair toss about.

The guards snickered, and Gandry winked at them.

Angwyn turned his attention to each young woman in the line again the wall. None looked up at him as they remained near statues. He stopped before one who was familiar. He used a gentle finger to raise her chin. This was the girl who Gwilim had taken from the meeting room and asked to help in the kitchen. Isabelle, he finally recalled her name. She was in the keep to work with the friar most days. Should he need a maid, it would be easy to collect her. "This one. She will do."

"A wonderful and wise choice, m'lord. I am sure she will prepare your room something artful."

Angwyn hoped the man was less of fool when sober, but somehow, he doubted it. "Now, get to your quarters, sergeant. That's an order."

Isabelle stepped from the other women as Angwyn made his way passed the group to continue down the short hall to his chamber. Did one of the women yelp softly?

Gandry's words covered much of the noise. "Well now, his lordship has *commanded* us back to our quarters." Even his mutter held evidence of his drunken smirk. "How convenient."

The other guards laughed. Angwyn almost thought some of the women whimpered and even began to cry.

Chapter 13

Din Osways, Scotland

Angwyn entered his orderly chamber with a satisfied sigh. All his trunks and been unpacked and removed to be stored somewhere else in the keep. Only those of Sintest's, containing his weapons and official papers, remained. He'd deal with them in the morning.

He undid his belt and placed his weaponry on one of the chairs. He drew off his outer short surcoat but remained in his shirt and hose. Shuffling behind him reminded Angwyn that he was not alone. Gracious, he was weary. He coughed again. It was custom among some nobility to have the chambermaid sleep within the noble's bedchamber. Angwyn wasn't one of them. He'd let Isabelle know what she could do to tidy his chambers each morning and send her to where all the other servants slept.

Movement near the door caught his eye and he turned to address her. "You may start with—"

Isabelle stared at the floor as she untied the closers down the front of her dress, preparing to disrobe.

He froze as his heart jolted. "Explain yourself!"

Isabelle clutched the front of her garment closed as she staggered back a step.

"You choose to insult me with this presumption?" he demanded. "However you bought your favors previously, I do not stoop to such debauchery. I should have you flogged."

The girl shuddered and backed away from him until she banged into his closed door.

He raised a stiff arm that quaked with the wrath he barely contained. "Out! Get out, now."

Isabelle almost doubled over as though he had punched her but they stood too far apart. Her Scottish words babbled from her trembling lips. "Feuch, aThighearna, chan eil."

His arm dropped to his side as he stared at her.

She tried again in English. "If ya send me out … thee others … thee other men—" Her words were drowned in her sobs as she slumped to the floor. Her hand clasped before her as she begged him through her tears. "Please, yar lordship. Please."

The image of the winking drunk men filled his mind. The women who coward against the wall—one for each of them. Those same men who had come into the dining hall the day he arrived, but not for food. They had stared at Isabelle hungrily. All of these images hit him at once. This was worse than debauchery. This was the worst kind of evil.

Angwyn snatched up his belt, and rushed past Isabelle as she scurried out of his way with a yelp. He secured his weapons around his waist again as he thundered down the stairs. Ramonth was nowhere in sight, but he spotted Hywel and a group of soldiers still at the tables.

He stomped past them on quick pounding strides. "Hywel, gather those men and follow me."

Gwilim tucked a stack of plates close to his chest and stepped out of his path with a wide gaze.

"Get those guards out of here and I want all ale sealed."

"My lord?"

As Angwyn charged across the small courtyard to the barracks, his soldiers hurried to keep pace with him. The sound of a harsh slap and a woman's yelp accompanied crying loud enough to be heard through the walls. It made every muscle in his body clench. He smashed the door open and it hit the wall with a boom.

Gandry had one of the women against the wall as he opened his pants. The other two men were removing their clothes as well. The sobbing women did little to fight back.

How many times had this happened to them to make them cower in the face of such despicable actions?

On three long pounding strides, Angwyn came to stand toe to toe with the inebriated ring-leader.

Gandry raised one brow as his lips curved in his lopsided drunken smirk.

"If you were not drunk beyond all reason, I would have you stripped and expelled for this." Perhaps he should do it anyway. But even as drunk as he was, and devoid of standing in the king's army, Gandry would still be a threat to the women in the village.

While Gandry stared at him unmoved—other than to sway—Angwyn turned to his soldiers. "Put them on the wall."

Hywel and his soldiers seized the three drunk guards and jerked them toward the door.

"A few hours in this night air should sober them up. And teach them a lesson of who is in charge." That they would make him a party in their wickedness was beyond his grasp. Never had he met men so debased of all morality.

As the men left, Angwyn turned to the three young women who clutched one another as they tried to control their tears. It would do nothing for his respect amongst the villages or his attempt to arrest authority over them to apologize to these whimpering girls.

Two of his men remained and stood watching from the doorway.

"This type of behavior from men under my command is never to be tolerated. I have no idea how Lord Sintest ran this keep. But this is never to happen again."

They snapped to attention and gave a quick nod.

He glanced at the maids. "Are you able to return home safely, or do I need to provide you with an escort?"

"We can manage, m' lord."

He nodded, stomped to the door, and stepped again into the chilling wind and growing fog of a damp and dreary night. It was not enough punishment for what those men had been about to do.

"Thank ya, m' lord," one of the women said as they skirted passed him toward the gate.

Angwyn met the remainder of those who had been in the hall as they staggered out. Some were so drunk they had to be supported by their friends. "Get to your quarters."

After a short search, Angwyn found Gwilim. "Is that the last of it?"

The stoic friar carried a keg of beer to a small lauder where he added it to the stacks of beer, ale, and wine. All the food had been removed, leaving only the alcohol. "Yes, my lord." Gwilim ducked under the lintel, stepped out of the small storage room, and closed the door. He flipped the iron slat over the hook sunk deep in the stone wall, placed a lock over it, and snapped it shut.

"I will hold the key," Angwyn reached out his hand and Gwilim dropped the cool metal into his palm.

He turned to find his captain standing crossed armed behind him. Ramonth arched his brows.

"This night will never happen again, captain. As I said before, get these men whipped into shape." He paused as he came alongside his captain. "And if a whip is required, don't use it sparingly."

With the key in his belt, his hands still fisted and unfisted as he stomped up the tower to his chamber—although it was a much slower ascent than earlier. He stepped inside his warm chamber with a deep sigh, again removed his weapons, and placed them on the chair. Candles were lit. His bed was turned down, inviting him to comfort and rest. His night shirt lay draped over the bottom corner of the bed.

Isabelle had remained after he'd stormed out. She now lay sleeping, curled on a small rug near the fire. The light of the dancing flames moved over her small form, giving it movement while the girl remained still. How many times had she suffered? She'd been willing to offer herself to him as though it was a common occurrence. Was there any wonder that the men of this land banded together to rebel again the English and their atrocities?

The fight and wrath from earlier melted out of him and left Angwyn drained. He was grateful Gwendolyn and the maids of his household had never suffered a similar fate. It would have driven him to a vengeful madness that he would never have recovered from.

At the thought of his love, Angwyn turned to the dried flowers she'd gifted him. He stepped to the table beside his bed and cradled them gently. He couldn't think of bringing her here until he had these deplorable men more under control. His thoughts traveled back to their early days together, to her gentle smile and full laughter. Oh, how he missed those days!

With a quick glance at Isabelle again, he slipped the token of his wife's continued affection into a keepsake box and set it high on a shelf in the bookcase near the door. He blew out all the candles but one before he finished undressing and donned his night shirt. He'd let Isabelle know tomorrow that she should stay with the other servants, but she'd had a trying evening and he didn't want to wake her.

He muffled another cough, blew out the last candle once he was in bed, and let the horrible day drift away. He even sent up a quick prayer that, with the coming of the dawn, things would change dramatically at Din Osways. Did God still listen to his infrequent prayers?

Chapter 14

Din Osways, Scotland

Ramonth trudged up the stairs to Lord Kenseth's chamber. He was already weary of the complaints of the men as they learned that all alcohol was off limits. He would have to talk to his friend about such harsh conditions. Was it not bad enough that they were in this bog?

A young woman stepped out from Kenseth's door and pulled it closed without even a click of the latch. She whirled around and sucked in a lung-full of air when she almost ran into him. It was the maid from the meeting room the day they had arrived. She ducked her head, dipped a small curtsy, and dashed around him down the stairs.

Ramonth would never have thought of Angwyn as one to indulge in the company of women. This place seemed to be having a strange effect on his lord.

He pushed open the lord's door as Kenseth threw off his covers and rose out of bed. He tried to keep the smirk off his face. It was nice to see Lady Gwendolyn's prudish values and religious tenants had little hold on his friend. Getting their drink back seemed like a definite possibility. "Good morning, my lord. Sleep well?"

Kenseth glanced around the room. He sighed when he found they were alone and nodded. So, he didn't want Ramonth to know he'd entertained the young woman. That was interesting.

Kenseth splashed water on his face and Ramonth dropped into one of the chairs. "The men are unhappy."

Kenseth reached for the towel. "After their horrid behavior last night, I care little for their happiness."

"They had a little drink. There was no harm." Ramonth stretched out his legs and crossed his ankles.

The towel hurtled next to the basin and Kenseth glared at him as his voice rose. "Tell that to the four women they abducted and intended to spoil."

What was Kenseth talking about?

While he dressed, and in between coughing, Kenseth gave Ramonth instructions of the training that he wanted the men to endure. It started with the hard labor of rebuilding the gangway on the roofs of the towers and the hall.

"You want our men to do this work?"

Kenseth nodded. "It is their punishment."

"But that is why we control a village full of hardened Scots. They should see to the labor and our men to their protection."

Kenseth whirled around on him, braced his hands on the table between them, and narrowed his eyes. "It is those villagers who need protection from these men. If you work them hard enough, then maybe they won't have the energy to rape young women."

"Rape?" Ramonth glanced at the door where Isabelle had exited moments before.

In short order, Ramonth followed his lord down the stairs and into the hall where the men sat hunched over their sparce fair for the early morning meal. Few spoke. Many of the guards glanced up and shot hateful gazes on Kenseth as he took his seat.

Ramonth lowered next to him and watched the men as Gwilim

rushed to bring them plates and cups of water.

Ramonth struggled to control his distain. "Your sobriety campaign seems to be having an effect."

"The men must know that the debauchery of last night will not be tolerated."

Ramonth considered his words from before. "None of it?"

"None." Kenseth barked the word as he thumped his cup down on the table.

"If you say so." It didn't seem right that he enjoyed the company of a woman and forbid the men.

Kenseth lowered the bit of salted fish he'd pinched between his fingers and turned to look at him. "There is a line, Inek. It was crossed. My sobriety and my loyalties may not align with every one of yours, but each one of these men needs to know—without a doubt—that I am in charge. I would hope I have your support in at least that."

Ramonth shrugged as he took a bite of cheese and chewed it before answering. "As long as that line lies in the same place for everyone, you have my full support. But, as you say, I am in charge of the men." He turned a raised a brow as he stared at Kenseth. "They will not respect one who applies rules unequally."

The lord's forehead creased and he pulled and he pulled back as if he had been slapped. "I make no rules that do not apply to everyone—"

The hall doors swung open and banged against the stone walls, which drew everyone's attention. The men fell silent as the two guards, Orion and Alistair, who were constantly in Gandry's shadow, entered the room. They led the large villager Ramonth had noticed the day before and the pretty woman who had stood beside him.

Leaving the two with Alistair, Orion worked his way past the tables and approached Kenseth as Ramonth at the front table. "They request a word with you, m' lord."

Ramonth didn't care for the way the man said Kenseth's title.

The lord glanced up at the couple and back at the guard. "Bring them to the meeting chamber."

"Yes, m'lord." Orion returned to the couple and Alistair and directed them along the back of the hall toward the chamber.

Kenseth stood and strode across the large chamber as the men finished their meal. Ramonth followed. Inside the smaller meeting chamber, the lord stepped over the dark stain on the floor as he went around the table and sat in the tall backed chair. Ramonth moved to stand beside him. He fiddled with his dagger, twisting it so it caught the light though the window. Best to let this big man know he'd protect his lord.

The woman stepped into the room. The man had to duck under the lentil. He stood almost a full head taller than Alistair, who tried to shove him further into the room. The hulking Scotsman didn't budge. He had broad shoulders, a muscled chest, and thick waist supported on sturdy legs that were currently set apart. His long hair was groomed into a warrior's knot above his collar, and though his beard was also long, it was neat and clean.

Orion stepped around him to push the woman forward, but one look from the Scotsman and the guard thought better of it.

Both guards moved a few steps back near the rear wall.

The couple stepped closer and stopped. They stood tall on the other side of the table, well out of sword reach. While it didn't look like the big man was armed, Ramonth knew better than to assume such.

Gwilim wiped his brow with the brown sleeve of his course robe. It may have been damp and, at times, even chilly in Scotland, but as a man working in the kitchens with a few squires, he was always hot.

He stepped from the stifling kitchen and into the cooler hall as the last of Lord Kenseth's soldiers ambled out. The breaking of the fast was frowned on this early in the morning in most households. But Lord

Kenseth thought the fighting men needed a bit of bread, cheese, and salted fish before they began their day. Between the light meal, the village visitors, and the prohibition on their much-loved drink, most had not lingered today.

He gathered another stack of plates. They were littered with food. He dumped the remains on one plate, put it on top of the stack, and carried them to the kitchen.

When he returned, Isabelle hurried through the doorway from the tower. "There you are." He'd hoped the girl would have been here earlier. Perhaps the Scots didn't favor an early meal either.

She stood by one of the uncleared tables and startled at his words. Her eyes widened as she took a step back.

Gwilim smiled as he approached and started gathering the plates. "I'm glad." He needed the help. If she could see to the cleaning of the dishes, he could focus on preparing the large midday dinner. "We can chat while you help me clean." He placed plates in her arms before he gathered a stack himself and turned to the kitchen. "On now. Follow me."

Now that he had help, this would be much easier. If not for the pile of tin in his arms, he might have danced into the hot kitchen. God was good.

Gwilim turned, but Isabelle had not entered behind him. He set his load down with the others he'd already brought in and returned to the hall. It was empty. He caught a glimpse of her skirt as the door out of the hall closed. The plates he'd given Isabelle were left on the table where they'd stood. None of the food remnants were there, however. The pile he put on the one plate was gone, and the little he'd noticed on the other plates had been cleaned off as well.

He glanced up at the closed door again. What had made her run off? And, now, what was he going to feed the pigs?

Chapter 15

Din Osways, Scotland

Angwyn sat behind the table in the meeting chamber and waited for the large man to inform him of his business in the coming to the keep. He didn't have to wait long.

"Lord Kenseth, I be York, thane of Din Osways. This be me wife, Ellen." The man's deep growling voice matched his appearance.

Angwyn nodded. So, the man Ramonth had thought they needed to be on guard for was the leader of the villagers. His captain had a discerning eye.

"We hev come here to apologize for the events of yesteern. The lad, Henric, he's a good lad, hard workin' an' all."

So, the boy who threw mud at him was Henric. A name Angwyn would not soon forget. He steeled his emotions and let York continue.

"He meant no harm by it. Lucky throw it were. Most times he'd hev more likely hittin' ground than—"

Ellen cleared her throat. Smart woman. She reminded Angwyn a lot of his wife. Both were handsome women even for their age, and they knew their men could get in a bit of trouble if left to their own devices.

"Right. As it be. We did brin' a gift. Isn't a whole much, but it be sincere. Baked by me wife just this morn.'"

Ellen held up the bundle of cloth in her hand. She opened it to reveal a few small rolls of bread inside.

Angwyn nodded to the table between them. York had spoken true. It wasn't much of a gift. But he gave the man credit for coming to him in person and addressing the incident.

Ellen placed the bread on the table as Angwyn stood. "York, is it?"

"Aye."

Now was his moment to claim his authority. If he could get York to submit, the rest of the town was likely to follow. "Well, York, Thane of Din Osways, you do not impress as a man foreign to conflict."

"Aye." York held his gaze unwavering. The men were coming to an understanding.

"You understand the rule of law and of order, or you would not be standing here before me this morning. This much is true. We cannot abide behavior that fosters disrespect of that order."

The hard tone of his voice, and tightness of his stance flagged. "We jus' wish ta live in peace, m'lord."

Angwyn drew in a deep breath and squared his shoulders. "You have an odd way of achieving it. The boy will be found and appropriately punished."

Ellen covered her gasp with the edge of the shawl draped around her.

"Lord—" York's voice vibrated.

"Your efforts to defend the boy are duly noted. But an example must be made." If Angwyn let this go without any consequences, the next to show him disrespect might do so with a dagger. Some action had to be taken. "You would do well to bring the boy with you next time we meet."

"Lord...?" This time, it was a quiet plea.

Angwyn nodded to the guards. He was done with Thane York and his wife.

York didn't move. "He be jus' a boy."

"All the more reason, York, Thane of Din Osways. The actions of your people fall on you. It is best you teach them the way things are. Then, and only then, can you have your peace. King Edward is your ruler now. The sooner that is accepted by all, the better off we will all be."

Angwyn stepped around the table toward the thane.

York straightened, taking the challenge for what it was. "We Scots be a proud people, Lord Kenseth. We'll comply with yar wishes, 'cause we must. As a man yarself, 'nay foreign to conflict,' ya would be aware that be very different from acceptance. I rule me people 'cause I hev earned their respect. Ya would be wise ta do the same."

York turned and led his wife from the meeting chamber and the guards followed.

Ramonth stepped beside him. "They're afraid."

Angwyn opened the bundle of bread. "As well they should be. My venture is that the boy is their son." He picked up a meager roll and brought it to his nose. It had a strong scent of herbs.

"Shall we take that advantage?" There was too much excitement in Ramonth's tone for his liking.

"As you said, they are already afraid. We cannot take that which we already have. The power of fear is an intoxicating drink, Inek. We have made our point. It is best not to overdo it." He took a bite of the bread and quickly felt something hard in his mouth. Could Ellen have tried to poison him? He drew out a small leaf and examined it. Rosemary. Harmless, but not something he favored in his bread.

Ramonth leaned closer to examine the foreign substance. "They put twigs in their bread?"

Angwyn shrugged and tossed the rest of the roll back with the others. His gaze shifted to the heaping bowl of English bread at the other end of the table. "The seasons are changing. Have the friar give us an inventory of our storehouse."

Ramonth nodded and moved toward the door to see to his tasks.

"Oh, and Inek … Gather some men. Search hard enough for the boy to make the villagers worried, but not so hard that you actually find him."

A wide grin spread across his captain's face. "Yes, my lord."

Between him and Inek, the villagers of Din Osways would fall in line. Of that, he had no doubt.

Chapter 16

Conwy, Wales

Gwendolyn couldn't contain her smile. Market days, when one had coin, were a spectacle best enjoyed with slow meandering. Unlike days when necessities must be found and purchased for the least amount of coin and in the shortest amount of time, today, she could linger and savor the rhythmic chaos of the many peddlers, hucksters, stallholders, and merchants.

Katlyn walked beside her as they left the castle walls and strolled to market square.

"'Tis a good day to visit the market." Gwendolyn sighed as a contented smile spread across her face.

"Yes, my lady."

"What treasures do you think we'll find today? Perhaps a bit of lace, or a new bobble for my hair?"

Her maid's gaze was elsewhere, and she bumped into Gwendolyn. Katlyn had to readjust the empty basket she held against her hip. "Pardon, my lady."

"We haven't even arrived at the square yet, Katlyn. There will be even more to see there." A child-like giddiness washed over Gwendolyn.

As they neared the market with its growing sounds, Gwendolyn whispered to Katlyn. "I am grateful for last evening's rain. It washed away some of the stench of the busy streets."

Katlyn smirked. "Yes, my lady. But there are still the unwashed peasants and the overly perfumed courtiers."

"Oh, and the scent of bakers' fresh breads, and the victuallers' pies and pastries. We must get pastries to nibble as we shop."

Again, Katlyn seemed distracted, but they stopped and purchased a small berry-filled treat.

"Chicken for your dinner, m'lady?"

Gwendolyn gasped at the squawking animal thrust at her by a peddler dangling it by its feet. The chicken flapped its wings and a few bits of down floated around her until she sneezed.

She waved the chicken aside and continued on.

"Bread, fresh bread!"

"Ribbons for your hair, ladies!" They stopped at the ribbon stand and looked, but with her hair under a wimple, and her gowns finely adorned already, she had no need for ribbons. In truth, living in Conwy Castle, she wanted for nothing.

"Pots." The stallholder banged a wooden spoon against the bottom of the black metal pot she held. "Strong pots fer all yer cookin' needs!"

"The finest pottery in all north Wales." A thin man with whisps of hair waved his hand over his wares. "Plates for yer table, bowls for yer stew, pitchers for yer wine. Surely ye need a bit of my pottery to adorn yer fine home, m'lady."

As Gwendolyn stopped to look at a small blue bowl perfect for holding her few pieces of jewelry, Katlyn bumped into her.

The maid startled. "Pardon, my lady."

"Where is your head today, Katlyn?" Gwendolyn purchased the small bowl and they moved along the lines of stalls as the shopkeepers shouted from their doorways. The woman at the tavern all but filled the entrance as she touted the quality of her ale.

"Lamb, fresh lamb, just slaughtered this morning." This man held a bloody section of ribs in the air.

Gwendolyn sidestepped the butcher. "I should remember to ask His Majesty what types of foods to expect in Scotland."

Katlyn again brushed against her, in her inattention. "Much the same, I imagine, my lady. We could always send a letter to your husband and ask."

"I've heard some horrible things about a dish they call haggis. Angwyn—Lord Kenseth—has never paid much mind to what food was set before him."

Again, Katlyn brushed up against her. It wasn't like the girl to be so distracted. "Then maybe the friar," Katlyn mumbled.

Gwendolyn selected some colored thread and a fine piece of linen to do some embroidery before her attention was drawn to a small table tucked between a metal worker and several peasants selling produce. On his table were many bundles of dried flowers. They brought to mind the small bouquet she'd gifted Angwyn the day he departed. Did he favor it? Did he look at it and think of her?

A boy in dirty trousers and shirt stood and smiled. He was a little younger than her dear William had been. "Greetin's, m'lady. May I assist?"

The joy of the day seeped from her as her thoughts swirled around her long dead child and her husband who had never recovered.

Katlyn stepped on Gwendolyn's toe.

Gwendolyn turned to reprimand the maid more sternly, but Katlyn's gaze was fixed elsewhere. Gwendolyn followed her nervous stare. Many of the shoppers were staring back at them. Faces she had seen in the castle and at the picnic watched her and then leaned close to talk together.

Nerves jingled inside her, and her stomach rolled around the pastry she'd sampled earlier as Gwendolyn's gaze was met by Lady Bess. The dour woman, who was a little younger than herself, glared back. Gwendolyn had overheard the noble English woman, more than once, speak against the Welsh and their lands in the most visceral of language.

Gwendolyn swallowed as she shifted her gaze back to the lad. "No, thank you, I believe we will be on our way."

She turned back toward the castle. "Come, Katlyn." Gwendolyn walked with slow purpose, head up, as she noted how many openly observed her passing. She huffed as she walked through the city gate and moved toward the castle. What caused such open hatred? It was not her fault that the king showed her favor. She'd done nothing to seek it out.

The summer sun now shone down from directly overhead as Katlyn walked beside her with the basket of Gwendolyn's purchases on her arm. "Please take care, my lady."

"What are you trying to say?"

"Nothing, my lady. I am just urging you to be cautious, that is all."

Katlyn was a mere servant. Where did she find the gall to caution her mistress? "I have done nothing wrong, and I will not be bullied by gossiping hags. His Majesty treats me no differently than any other member of his court."

Kaylyn released a small sigh. "Yes, my lady."

Gwendolyn jerked to a stop and placed her hands on her hips as she whirled on the insolent maid. "You will watch your tone and learn your place."

Katlyn at least had the good sense to lower her head before she responded. "Pardon, my lady. I only wish—"

"And you will keep your wishes to yourself." She threw her arms straight at her sides and started walking again. Katlyn hurried to keep pace with her mistress' quick steps.

Perhaps it was time to make arrangements to join Angwyn.

Chapter 17

Din Osways, Scotland

C lutching the folds of her skirt, Isabelle wound through the trail outside the village. The events of last night tumbled in her head. The new English lord wasn't like the others. Their priest, who at least tried to speak Gaelic—though not well—had saved her once from the Gandry and his brutes, but when Muire, Eilidh, Ailis, and she had been pulled from the villages last night, she'd been angry and terrified. The men were so drunk. She had bruises on her arms. But it could have been so much worse.

As she climbed a small rise, she rubbed away the gooseflesh at the memory of how angry the lord had been when she'd started to take her clothes off. It was why the men had forced her to his door. It was why he'd picked her—or so she'd thought. But the lord hadn't understood at all. He threatened her, but then he must have realized what Gandry and the scum with him had wanted.

Isabelle's heart still skipped a beat of the thought of him picking up his weapons and charging toward her. But he'd left. And he never touched her. She'd tidied his room, turned down the many blankets on his big bed, added wood to the fire, and curled next to it. She hadn't moved when he returned. He'd undressed in near darkness and slipped into bed. Even with his refusal to take her, and his anger at the thought, Isabelle still hadn't been able to fall asleep until the lord started to snore.

"Got'cha, Surrender!" Henric leapt out from behind a clump of brush and pointed a stick he'd whittled into a mock sword at her belly.

She pushed it aside and scowled at her brother. "Ain't ya already in enough trouble?"

"I be a rebel, fightin' for thee honor of thee Scots." Henric slashed the useless weapon through the air between them.

Isabelle shook her head and rolled her eyes. Her brother may have passed his tenth summer, but he was still such a child. She sat on a rock poking out of the ground and opened the pocket of fabric she'd created by pinching together the front of her skirt.

Henric snatched up a slice of bread and plopped down on the damp grass next to her. His sword slid through the air and poked at the dirt as he ate more of the remains of the soldiers' morning meal.

"They be lookin' for ya, ya keen."

Henric pointed the dull tip of his stick-sword at her. "Let 'em look. They can nay catch me."

"They caught Da." Isabelle remembered the day the English soldiers had dragged York from their home, and the way she and muther cried. She'd been surprised he'd returned. Da was bloody, but they hadn't killed him. Now, there was a new English lord. Henric had thrown mud at him and now the lord's men searched. Would Henric only suffer a beating, or might this lord spare him like he had her?

Henric finished what he was chewing and grabbed the last scrap of fish from her lap. He could have it. "That were different," he said as he tipped back his head and dropped the salty morsel in his mouth.

Isabelle brushed the crumbs from her lap. "I dinae think Da would think so. Why does he stay here instead of joinin' with the rebels?"

"I dinae keen. I reckoned he were just old." Henric shrugged and licked his fingers clean as his gaze turned to the village a little below them.

Isabelle followed his gaze as her brother watched the tall priest in his brown long tunic march to the village entrance. These new comers were certainly strange. Their priest had to be the oddest among them though. He looked more like Da, or the soldiers who had come with the new lord. Tall and covered in muscles his brown robe strained to control, he barked orders and commanded those under him, but he'd smiled at her and been gentle in his request that she help with the cooking. She watched as he waved at those he met.

Henric moved to a crouch and pressed his finger across his lips for her to be quiet.

She shook her head and tried to grab his arm, but her little brother was quick. He darted through the brush, down the hillside, and slipped inside the village behind the large man. Isabelle stood. She glanced at the stone castle casting a shadow over her home—in more ways than one. The lord had picked her as a maid, and he seemed to only want her to clean his rooms. The priest wanted her help in the kitchen—but at the moment, he was in the village being stalked by her brother.

She glanced at the village again. Best go see what trouble Henric was going to get into this time. There was no chance of stopping him.

Keeping to the shadows, she watched Gwilim stroll along. He stared at their near-empty harvest baskets, watched some women mending tattered garments with what little supplies they had, and, yet, he greeted each with kindness and terrible Gaelic.

Isabelle stifled a groan.

Henric leapt out in the man's path and ordered the Englishman not to pass. "Cha téid thu seachad." Henric held his mock sword with both hands as he pointed it at the priest.

Gwilim stood at attention and acknowledged Henric with a nod. "Greetings. Where did you come from?" The alert man scanned round with a sharp gaze as if he searched for where Henric had popped out of, or if anyone accompanied him. "I'm—"

Henric darted forward and swung his sword.

Thunk.

The priest dropped to the ground and Isabelle covered the scream her tight throat wouldn't allow to escape. Her brother was already being hunting for attacking the new lord. Now, he'd just struck the powerful man's priest. They'd kill him for sure.

The large man remained motionless on the ground. No one moved as the entire village seemed to hold its breath. How could Henric be so foolish?

Leather creaked and mail rattled behind her. The lord's men were riding their big horses into the village. Isabelle's heart pounded in her ears. She couldn't draw in a breath as the man in front, the lord's thane, spied Henric standing over their holy man lying still on the ground. In only a heartbeat, they kicked their horses to charge at her brother.

Henric darted between buildings where the horses couldn't follow.

"You three, head that way." The thane pointed. "You men go there. Head the little trouble maker off. Don't let him escape again."

The man didn't follow the other soldiers. He glanced down at the priest as Gwilim groaned, rubbed his head, and tried to sit up.

"Welcome back," the thane said with a smirk.

Gwilim rose up on both elbows with another moan. "This must be how Christ felt when he rose from the grave." He balanced on one elbow and rubbed his head again.

"If I remember the stories, your Christ didn't get clocked by a ten-year-old with a stick."

Gwilim glance up at the man. "My Christ, all knowing and supreme, didn't have to worry about a surprise attack, Captain Ramonth."

The captain straightened in his saddle and narrowed his eyes on the holy man still lying in the dirt. "Seems to be your life story."

The priest huffed. "I have paid my price for that day a thousand time over, captain."

The captain reached down a hand at last. "Aye, we all have, my friend. But some more than others."

Gwilim took the offered hand with a grunt and rose to his feet. Isabelle slipped away and headed toward home. She wondered what day the two Englishmen referred to and why they both believed they were being punished for it. Did the English ever get paid back for the bad they did? It didn't seem like it.

She didn't see or hear the soldiers searching for her brother. Henric was good at hiding and slipping though small places. But his luck would run out one day and he'd pay for all this trouble he was causing the English. Her people *always* paid.

Chapter 18

Din Osways, Scotland

Angwyn rubbed his temple at the dull ache growing into a throbbing annoyance. Why had he let Gwendolyn convince him to bring this confounding friar?

Unfortunately, he'd barely sat down before Gwilim had marched in with Ramonth on his heel. Angwyn gripped a kerchief and his stomach rolled as the man prattled on about the poor conditions of the villagers. He noted again the raised lump on the man's wide forehead. Why was it that Angwyn's own head ached, though Gwilim was the one who'd suffered a blow?

Blinking his eyes, Angwyn focused on the man's words again. "Trade? What are you talking about?"

Gwilim nodded. "Yes, my lord. *We* have an abundance. *Our* stores are full. We have a stockyard of pigs and fowl for eggs."

Angwyn glanced at his captain. Ramonth sighed and shrugged his shoulders as Angwyn returned his attention to Gwilim with a sigh. "Go on."

"The sow has recently birthed us nine piglets." The mighty friar held up nine fingers as if Angwyn didn't know how many piglets that was and needed a visual to understand.

Angwyn stared at the man. "That's all well and good, friar, but you still have not explained to me what you were doing in the village by yourself."

Gwilim tipped his head and furrowed his brow as his hands dropped to his sides. "Is it not the calling of the church to reach *all* peoples, my lord?"

Angwyn leaned back in his chair. "It was not the church who had to ride in and save you today." His stomach rolled again.

Gwilim's mouth dropped open and he huffed as he threw his shoulders back.

Angwyn didn't give him leave to protest. "What you fail to understand here, friar, is our stores are full because the villagers pay us."

The friar's hands reached outward with his palms up. "For *what*, my lord?"

"For protection," Angwyn said.

Gwilim narrowed his gaze. "From whom, my lord?"

Ramonth straightened. "Brother Gwilim, do not press your position. You know why we are here."

Ramonth rarely acknowledged the friar by his religious title. Angwyn glanced between them again. Did they conspire together?

Gwilim looked to the captain. "I know why *you* are here."

Ramonth widened his stance and crossed his arms. So, perhaps they were not colluding together.

Angwyn stood and braced himself against the table top. "The fact is, it does not matter if you like why we are here or if the villagers like why we are here. Our soldiers must be paid. We must be paid. You must be paid."

The friar pressed his hand to his chest. "I?"

"Our king must be paid," Angwyn continued.

Now, Gwilim crossed his arms. "So, we tax them to protect them from ourselves. A service they neither asked for or desire. And then what? These people—your people—"

Angwyn stood tall. "My people?" He didn't care for this man—of all men—reminding him all he had similarly experienced under this king. His people were back in Wales. They had suffered the English lords taxing them in the name of protection too. Now, he was one of them doing the same to these Scots.

Gwilim leaned forward. "Whose people do you think they are?"

They were not—never would be—*his* people. Angwyn was here only to restore his own name. Perhaps when he'd completed his duty to the king here, he could then use his new status to help *his* people—the Welsh. "Watch your words, friar."

"My words?" Gwilim raised his chin and narrowed his gaze. "You call yourself lord. You walk around these halls, all the while ignoring what lies about. Yes, *your* people. We have taken away their dignity, denied them any other leader. And for what? A king they have never seen and never wanted? I have taken a vow to serve, Lord Kenseth. A vow to serve my God. It will forever supersede any edict or command from any king, or from you, for that matter. If you take exception to that, I suggest you take it up with Him." He raised his finger to point heavenward. "It would do you some good."

There it was again. The guilt of putting these people under the same suffering as he endured. Angwyn stepped out from behind the table and stalked toward the friar. "You come into my keep and have a roof over your head at the bequest of my wife. Not I." Yet again, he regretted acquiescing to his wife wishes. "Do not forget that. And, yes, I will take it up with *your* God. I have taken it up with Him every day since my son was taken. If you take exception to *that*, then possibly it is *you* and not I who needs to have that conversation with *Him*." Angwyn leaned in so he was almost nose to nose with the man. "And until that day, I will rule as I see fit. I will not be instructed on the subject, by you or any other of your ilk."

Ramonth eased the two apart and stepped between them. "Gentlemen, please. We are Welsh and can deal with our disagreements with more calm."

Angwyn spun back to the table.

"My lord—"

Ramonth cut him off. "Brother Gwilim."

The friar sighed. "My pardon, Lord Kenseth. I have overstepped. Please forgive me. I will do as you wish. My pardon."

Of course he would do as Angwyn wished; he had no other choice. Angwyn closed his eyes and drew in a deep breath. *A king they never wanted ... pay us to protect them from ourselves ...* So much like home.

His mind drifted to those first years under the English lords. What would it have been like for them to treat the Welsh with benevolence instead of derision? "Conduct your "trade," friar. But do not run out our stores or it will be your neck."

Gwilim inclined his head. "Thank you, my lord." Before Angwyn could change his mind or curtail the friar's behavior more, Gwilim turned and marched from the chamber.

Angwyn glanced to his captain. "Keep an eye on him."

Ramonth smiled and nodded. "Yes, my lord."

After a few days, the repairs of the gangway and roofs were almost complete. Angwyn stood on the battlements and surveyed the men's progress. The men had been surly at first but they finally settled and got the job done.

A rider entered the courtyard below. He handed something to Ramonth, who turned and glanced up at Angwyn. Ramonth waited to have Angwyn's attention, before he waved something in his hand.

Angwyn raised his hand acknowledging he'd seen Ramonth and turned toward the stairs. They met in the meeting room and Ramonth handed Angwyn the letter.

He scanned the information quickly. He had yet to convince the people of Din Osways of his rightful place. This was not good news. "Gather me a detachment and supplies."

Ramonth arched a brow as Angwyn handed him the letter. Ramonth scanned the information for moment. "What's in Scone?"

"Apparently—" he pointed to the letter still in his captain's hands— "the other lords want to meet me."

"Well, aren't you popular."

Yes, too popular. He'd prefer to get his own house in order before he was called off to prove himself to a group of English noblemen. "Just keep everything standing while I'm gone, will you?"

Ramonth smirked. "I'll promise you *I* won't burn it down. Beyond that, no guarantees."

Angwyn allowed a short chuckle, glad for his friend's humor. "Then, not burning it down will have to do."

Ramonth nodded, passed back the letter, and turned to leave.

Chapter 19

Din Osways, Scotland

Gwilim stepped out from the storehouse and into the busy yard. Lord Kenseth's soldiers were finishing their preparations for his journey.

Surplus wheat, kale, hemp, wool ... Gwilim ran the list through his mind. He dodged soldiers carrying items to a wagon. Would the lord take the salted fish with him or should he add it to the list of items to trade? Gwilim should have been preparing the day's meal.

He turned toward the hall. What Gwilim really needed was some help. *Lord, You have supplied enough to feed us here in the keep and to aid Your children in the village. Help me find a way to tend to my responsibilities here and arrange for the trade—*

He spotted a young woman with a black braid swinging across her back. She entered the hall several steps ahead of him. Isabelle. He smiled. *Lord, You know my need before I even ask.* If he could get her to stay for more than a moment, Gwilim could have her start the meal preparation, while he loaded a wagon with some of the surplus goods.

Gwilim pounded up the stairs and marched into the hall. Isabelle stood still in the middle of the large room. He followed her gaze to see Gandry.

The guard swayed in a tunic that was near soaked through with sweat. The guard worked at the lock of the small store room that held the ale, beer, and wine barrels. He turned at the noise behind him. Gandry's eyes darted about, and the pry bar in his hand shook. More sweat dripped from his face. Gandry's frantic gaze landed on Isabelle and narrowed. "You."

Isabelle backed away. Gandry raised the heavy metal bar over his head and stalked toward her on unsteady steps. But the guard spotted Gwilim. Their gazes locked and Gandry stopped.

Though Gwilim knew the answer, he thought it best to draw the man's attention away from the young woman. "What is happening here?"

"None of your business, friar." Gandry drew a trembling arm across his face to wipe away the sweat dripping into his eyes.

Gwilim walked toward him to put himself between the guard and Isabelle. "You are in my hall. Therefore, I say it is my business."

Gandry raised the pry bar again, now directed at Gwilim. "And I say it is not." He lurched forward.

Gwilim seized his wrist with the weapon in one hand and punched the guard in the gut with the other. As Gandry doubled over, Gwilim twisted his wrist behind him and shoved him face first into the floor. Gwilim wretched the pry bar out of the guard's hand and dropped it on the man's back. Straightening, Gwilim stepped between the prone guard and Isabelle as he crossed his arms.

Gwilim glared down at Gandry as the man struggled to sit back on his heels and rub his arm. "I don't believe we have been properly introduced, sergeant. Brother Gwilim ap Gruffudd, formerly known, before my acceptance into the church of England, as Captain ap Gruffudd of the Welsh forces. You see dear man, I have already fought in more battles than you will ever survive. So yes, my hall, my business. Now, unless you have a legitimate reason for being in my hall, get out, before I choose to report you to his lordship, or maybe just take care of you myself."

Gandry huffed and lumbered to his feet. He brushed off the reeds and wove his way out the door.

Gwilim followed his movements until he was out of sight, and then shifted his gaze to Isabelle.

She stared at him wide-eyed and leaned away from him.

Gwilim lowered is voice to speak in a gentle whisper. He didn't move any closer to her so he would frighten her further. "Isabelle, my dear, you are just the person I was looking for. I need your assistance." He waved her toward the kitchen.

Angwyn finished tying his bed roll to the back of his saddle. Hywel and two more of his soldiers were already mounted and ready to travel.

He'd barely had time to settle in the keep and, already, he had to travel to Scone. What did the other lords want with him so soon?

Ramonth stood beside him. "I'll make sure the friar doesn't leave our stores empty."

Movement caught Angwyn's attention, and he raised his head to watch Gandry stagger out of the hall with a pry bar in his hand.

His captain followed his gaze. "You sure you don't want me to burn it down?"

"Yes." Angwyn mounted and settled into his saddle. "Just keep it civil. If the villagers give you any trouble, you know what to do. Short of that, keep both sides in line until my return."

Ramonth saluted and stepped aside as Angwyn turned his horse toward the gate.

Angwyn coughed and glanced at the sky as they neared the village. Rain clouds darkened the horizon and he sighed.

Chapter 20

Scone, Scotland

Angwyn rode northeast through rolling green hills for the better part of the day and arrived in Scone in the heart of the afternoon. He'd been grateful the storm followed them but never did more than darken the sky. The large city was said to have been the seat of the Scottish kings. In many ways, it reminded him of his home of Conwy. Built next to the River Tay, the city received many of its goods and people by ship. As the party drew near their destination, he found one major difference.

"That is not a castle, my lord," Hywel said.

"No, it is not."

As they approached, the long, gray two-story holy building rose out of the dark green landscape. The church was in a typical cross shaped design with a tall spire over the cross point. Its many windows looked down on them. Angwyn shook off the notion of the windows representing God's disapproving gaze as he passed beneath them.

He turned his attention from the scowling church to the ringed mound opposite. Moot Hill was said to be the place where the kings of Scotland finished their coronations before large crowds of their people.

They turned at the west end of the church and proceeded to the two-story building sprawling out behind it. Grooms came to tend the animals as squires stepped forward to lead them into the building. While two of his soldiers tended his belongings, Angwyn was allowed a moment to wash and a bit of refreshment. The beer was some of the finest he had ever had. The monks here were quite skilled in their brewing arts.

When he finished, Angwyn was directed to follow a couple of English lords down a long corridor running parallel to the huge hall. They turned into a room like the meeting chamber in Din Osways, only more than double in size. A long rectangular table filled the center and many lords were taking their places around it. Every man inside was English, save Angwyn, who was the only Welsh among them. What did that say of him, and Edward's appointment for this position? Did the king truly restore his honor, or was there something else behind him being the only Welsh man here?

A lord took the seat next to Angwyn as servants lined the walls ready to jump to serve the lords. "Welcome to Scotland, friend Angwyn." The man's brown wavy hair hung to his collar and grayed at his temples. A wide nose dominated his face, and he had a rather large forehead. But he smiled and offered Angwyn a nod in greeting.

Angwyn nodded back. "You have me at a disadvantage, sir."

"My pardon. Lord Finon of Stirling. The jewel of the land. Please, call me Richard."

Angwyn remembered passing the high perched fortified Stirling Castle on his way to Din Osways. Richard must have been quite favored by Edward to have acquired such a formidable holding. "Well met, Richard."

A lord dressed in dark green with short brown hair banged on the far end of the table.

"Lord Gresham," Richard whispered.

"Order! Order. I call this meeting of the lords to order." Gresham's deep voice rumbled through the room and the lords quieted. Gresham's gaze tuned on Angwyn. "Greetings to our newest arrival, Lord Kenseth of Din Osways. May Lord Sintest forever rest in peace."

The other lords pounded their fists on the table in agreement.

"This day, my brothers, shall go down in history," Gresham continued. "Today, we unite as one to finish what we have begun. John Balliol rots in the tower of London. We have won the war. It is time to reap the spoils!"

Angwyn joined the others as they cheered and thumped the table. He was caught up in being counted among the nobility again. Men-at-arms fighting for a common goal, their fervor and camaraderie stirred a starving part of his soul.

"We unite against the rabble." Gresham's voice rose in volume as did the answering cheers.

"We unite against the rebellion."

The growing cheers revibrated in Angwyn's chest quickening his heart. How he had missed this brotherhood.

"We unite for the king."

Angwyn's heart stuttered. It was harder to cheer for this.

"For England. To drive these Scots from this land."

As the room erupted in a cacophony of shouted cheers, Angwyn couldn't join them. Was this what they had done when they prepared to take Wales from his people? Had they been so excited to steal his land and his title? His stomach churned. Where was the honor in this?

Din Osways, Scotland

Ramonth tapped his foot as Gwilim fiddled with the lock. His throat was parched and the men were surly after several days with no proper drink.

"I don't believe Lord Kenseth would approve." The friar paused to glance at him with a scowl.

"Lord Kenseth left me in charge."

Gwilim turned and crossed his arms. "*I* do not approve."

Ramonth words added to the pounding in his head. "And what is it you don't approve of? We aren't opening the whole thing. Just getting one barrel out for tonight's meal. That big book of yours says something about not being drunk, does it not?" It was times like this Ramonth was grateful for his tutelage in religion. The right verse worked well to get those who followed the many lofty tenants to do what he wanted. If this one didn't work, he could always remind the troublesome friar Jesus Himself was said to have made wine.

It didn't look like it would be necessary as Gwilim's arms dropped to his sides and he sighed. "Paul's letter to the Ephesians, 'Do not be drunk with wine—'"

Ramonth drew the friar's attention back to the lock with a wave of his hand. "Well, there you have it, don't you? If you still have issue with it, get out the mead instead. Besides, drunk ain't the same as being only slightly snockered." Which was exactly the state Ramonth hoped to soon find himself. If Gwilim would just hurry up.

"It is in the intention of the deed where the evil is found sleeping."

Ramonth kneaded the muscles in his neck. "Well, my intention is to keep these men from rebelling while I am in charge. My apologies to your higher power, but I fail to see the evil in that."

"One barrel."

"One barrel," Ramonth agreed with a nod and the friar finally turned back to the lock.

Scone, Scotland

Angwyn ate little of the evening meal in near silence among the other excited lords and retired to his chamber early as the sporadic cough annoyed him, but sleep eluded him. When it came at last, it was accompanied by cheers and the battle cry of men ready to take the land —his land; his home; Wales.

Chapter 21

Scone, Scotland

Angwyn splashed water on his face and rubbed his hands over it. After the rally cry against the Scots, the talk of the previous evening had turned to the plan for rutting out and destroying the rebels and the taking and dividing of the land. He'd done his best to participate; he'd listened and memorized the plan of attack, but all of it had set at odds in his spirit.

Angwyn rubbed the towel slowly over his skin. He was glad for the meeting's location now being in a holy house. There would be no early breaking of the fast. The thought of food turned his stomach at the moment. He thought about entering the church to seek God for a moment. But, then, wasn't it God who had brought all this same devastation now planned for the Scots down on the heads of Angwyn and his people? Perhaps God wasn't the answer this time either.

After some time wandering the grounds around Scone Abbey, Angwyn returned to the hall in the late morning for the meal. The hall was full and noisy. With all the lords, their retainers, guards, those who worked and served the monks, and the monks themselves the large room was full.

Lord Richard Finon, waved him over and he set on the bench beside the man with a small group of lords. Richard raised his tankard to Angwyn as he set. It swayed slightly. Richard's eyes were rimmed red, and his smile was a little too big.

Richard took a draft and thumped the tankard down as he spoke loudly to the dark-haired man across the table. "No. Learn your history, man. Edward. *He* took the stone right back to England, where he could lord it over them."

Angwyn had heard the tale as he explored today. The Scots had some important stone that all their kings were crowned upon. Edward had taken it to Westminster Abbey about the same time Sintest had taken over rule of Din Osways.

Richard pointed an unsteady finger toward the front of the room. Angwyn's heart clinched painfully at the sight of the lean man surrounded by lords. He'd lost much of his hair, and what was left was gray. But Angwyn would never forget that face. The man still wore his beard trimmed to a point juking out from his chin. Add that to his pointy nose and small eyes and the man looked like the evil one incarnate.

Richard's voice tumbled in Angwyn's ears as they both looked at the man. "Now, that man over there. That is John de Warenne. Get to know him."

Angwyn knew more of the man than he ever cared to. He'd ridden beside Edward *that* day. He'd killed one of Angwyn's men as he and King Edward had come to demand his submission that day. And he'd glared at Angwyn and Ramonth as they'd taken their knees in surrender. He'd stood proudly beside his king as commander while Angwyn learned of his fate. It was only a testament to God's lack of favor that Angwyn was ever brought face to face with John de Warenne again. "Yes," Angwyn grumbled "Governor Warenne and I have met."

"Defeated the Scots at Dunbar," Richard said with admiration.

Angwyn downed half his drink and muttered into his tankard, "And the Welsh at Dolwyddelan."

"What was that?" Richard leaned forward trying to hear over the nose in the room.

"Nothing." Angwyn pulled his attention from the governor and looked back at Richard. "Just more of that *history* you were talking about."

They turned their attention to the food, but Angwyn struggled to eat, fearing the knots in his gut would only bring anything he managed to get down right back up again. He listened with disinterest to Richard and the others nearest them.

A door burst open at the back of the room with a shout. Heads throughout the hall turned and everyone quieted at the sight of a gasping, dirty soldier in the doorway.

The young man gulped air before he shouted. "Lord Bere is dead! Attacked, just outside of Kinross."

The lords rose from their meal without another word and charged from the room. Angwyn joined them as they pressed together to surge through the door and out to their horses. His heart pounded in his ears, caught up in the odd thrill that came before a battle. The mixture of excitement to prove one's prowess combined with the possibility of impending death now churned with his feeling for de Warenne, and the rightness of conquering the Scots. It was a heady concoction that left Angwyn unable to do more than follow the crowd and soak in their fervor.

Angwyn stood with his men as they prepared their horse. Intent on their tasks, none of them spoke.

Governor de Warenne charged to the center of the chaos of men preparing for battle. "To arms, men!"

Angwyn refused to turn and acknowledge that man as he continued to work. What did de Warenne think they were doing? Getting ready for an afternoon hunt?

"Let not one of these rabble go unpunished." De Warenne whirled away.

Within mere moments, all are mounted. The lords lined up with their soldiers behind them. De Warenne surveyed them and turned his mount toward Angwyn on his left. He rode up to stare at Angwyn like he had the day he'd taken a knee. "How is your blade, Lord Kenseth?"

Angwyn drew it from the sheath with slow purpose. How dare this man doubt his resolve to follow as he'd sworn an oath to do.

"Just make sure it is pointed in the *right* direction." De Warenne whirled his horse and led as they charged away from the abbey.

Angwyn returned the blade to its sheath as he watched the other lords and their men ride off after him. What had de Warenne meant? Did he accuse Angwyn of treason? By what grounds?

He spurred his horse forward, not to be left behind and have his honor called further into question. The exchange with the governor left him rattled and only added to the tumultuous emotions rolling inside of him. This was no way to go into battle. A man so distracted would end up dead. Had that been de Warenne's intention?

Angwyn focused on the drumming of the horses' hooves as they charged back the way he'd come toward the town of Kinross. His heart beat as loud as the hooves over the ground. Past battles filled his thoughts, and for a moment he saw *that* day again. The last image to greet him before they gained the city was of his dear Gwendolyn. Her eyes were filled with tears.

Chapter 22

Kinross, Scotland

The smell of charred wood filled Angwyn's nostrils and smoke stung his eyes. Not a building in the village of Kinross still stood. The bodies of men lay scattered where they had fallen, the stench of their deaths adding to the vile odors.

Soldiers taunted wailing women and crying children. The men yelled about the might of England and the fall of Scotland.

Angwyn surveyed it all from the saddle. His hand was slick with blood where he still held his sword.

A Scotsman was run through a few feet away, one of the last.

De Warenne rode up beside him. "Welcome to Scotland. Damn this land, and its climate."

Angwyn glanced toward the sky, noting for the first time the dark encroaching clouds. The governor's words from before they left still rang in Angwyn's ears. He raised his sword. "For the glory of the king!"

De Warenne turned and rode off without even a nod to Angwyn's salute.

He had followed the governor into battle and killed those supposedly responsible for a fellow lord's death. Why did it all sit at odds within him to fulfill his duty as charged by the king?

Movement to his left caught his eye. Angwyn turned to look at a boy covered in dirt. Streams of his tears made rivers of mud down his cheeks. The lad was younger than William had been.

Angwyn lowered his sword to rest on his thigh.

The men rode away from Kinross at a slower pace. Some of the seasoned regulars talked of those they had slain, each trying to outdo his companion with either the number of his kills or the difficulty. The younger soldiers who had just seen their first battle—slaughter would be a better word—rode wordlessly, staring ahead of them but not truly seeing.

Governor de Warenne drew between Angwyn and Lord Finon. "Yes, we have much work left to do. I hear the rebels are gathering forces again. Our victories have been many but these Scots just don't seem to know when they are beaten."

Unlike the Welsh, who gave in so quickly, Angwyn heard unspoken in the silence that followed. He kept his gaze straight ahead. "I suppose until you believe it yourself, you are not really beaten, are you?" Again, *that* day came to mind.

"And you? Are you *beaten?*"

Angwyn's grip tightened on his reins. Again, the man called him a traitor. "I am loyal to the crown and what is best for all, if that is what you are asking."

"You were granted this post, Lord Kenseth, at *my* recommendation."

His recommendation. For what purpose? Angwyn turned to look at the governor directly. What sport did the man play with his life?

"I expect you to be at *my* side when the battle begins. And it will begin."

Where else did this man think Angwyn would be?

Before he could ask, they came to a crossroad and de Warenne turned to the lane heading south toward England. "From here I head back home. It is time I plan before it begins again."

In truth, Angwyn was glad to be rid of him. "Safe travels to you." They each gave a salute as de Warenne and his detachment proceeded south. Angwyn followed Richard and the others heading in the other direction. What was the point of the man's messages? Why couldn't he be clear? Angwyn had fought today as ordered. He'd come to take control of Din Osways, as ordered. What made the governor suspicious of his allegiances?

Angwyn would need to be on his guard to assure no one found him wanting.

"You, Lord Kenseth, were not here during the fight to liberate this land." Richard's words drew Angwyn from his thoughts. Angwyn had forgotten the man rode beside him now that de Warenne had departed. Richard sighed. "Having been granted a land you did not have to fight for, we would not expect you to understand."

Was that the governor's point? He'd been given something he hadn't earned so he needed to prove himself like the others already had. It wasn't his fault he hadn't been called to the battle before now. "I heard the Scots left Stirling with just one footman behind to hand you the keys." If that was true, Richard hadn't fought for *his* holding either.

"Well, yes, but he was an awfully fierce footman."

There was silence for a heartbeat as the two stared at one another. Then, another beat went by and they both laughed heartily.

They reined in at another crossroads. Angwyn let the roiling thoughts of the day go as he smiled at a man he was quickly coming to like. "Well met, sir. And safe travels."

Richard smiled back and tossed him a leather wineskin. "From the spoils. The Scots left us a cellar full of French wine. Very courteous of them, if you ask me."

"I shall make good use of it."

The two men saluted. "Until our next meeting," Angwyn said.

Richard nodded as he turned his troops west toward the lane that would lead him back to Stirling.

Angwyn slipped the wine skin away as he turned his men east back to Din Osways with a cough. It was not Conwy, but it was home for now and he would be glad to see it again.

Chapter 23

Din Osways, Scotland

Angwyn rolled his shoulders and smiled as the tops of the towers of Din Osways poked out of the horizon. The ride back had been relatively short and blessedly dry. A half a league outside the village, movement in a gully to his left caught his attention. It was probably a hare or some other woodland animal.

When it flashed again, Angwyn took to staring at the grass-covered stream bank running alongside the road. If it had been an animal, it would have run from the noise of him, his men, and their horses.

Angwyn was rewarded with a glimpse of the lad who had thrown mud in his face. Henric. This time, the lad had nowhere to run. The deep stream gully had no trees or shrubs nearby, and they could easily outrun him on horseback if he tried to make it to the village.

Hywel pointed to signal that he'd seen the lad too. Angwyn gave him a nod as he halted the men. They grew quiet at the sudden stop so close to their destination. Angwyn drew the wineskin Richard had given him from his pack as he press a finger to his lips.

Hywel smiled as the other returned to their conversations.

Angwyn and Hywel dismounted and strolled to the deep ravine smiling at one another. The soldier drew his sword quietly, with a small nod. Angwyn moved his surcoat around, causing the fabric to rustle as if lifting it to relieve himself.

Henric lay pressed against the side of the stream bank a few feet below him. Angwyn could only see the top of his head. He uncorked the wineskin and let a steam of the clear white wine flow out on the lad's head. He gave the boy credit for not leaping up. Henric remained as still as stone as the liquid continued to soak him. It was a waste of good wine, but it was so worth it.

Angwyn suppressed his chuckle as he slowed and finally stopped the flow on the lad. He recorked the skin and turned back to the horses. His men watched, chuckling quietly as he and Hywel remounted.

"I feel so much better now," Angwyn said loud enough for the hiding lad to hear. He spurred his horse forward and they continued toward the village and the keep beyond. Though he glanced back often, he never saw Henric leave his hiding place. Angwyn's laughter couldn't be contained, though it was interrupted by an occasional cough.

He was still laughing a quarter hour later as they rode up the fortified ramp and through the keep gates. Neil, the young page, took the reins of his horse as he dismounted and Angwyn suffered a full coughing fit. The damp air in this country did no favors for his lungs.

Ramonth approached on long strides. "Welcome, my lord. The keep is still standing, as promised."

"Well done, captain."

Gwilim stepped from the hall with an ale barrel on his shoulder. By the single arm holding it in place, the container appeared to be empty. Before Angwyn could question it, Gwilim whirled and re-entered the hall and Ramonth stepped in his line of sight, hiding the friar and whatever he was up to.

"What word from the other lords?" Ramonth drew his attention, but they would discuss this later.

"Much to talk about. I fear this war is not as over as many of them seem to think." He coughed again as he turned to the hall to follow Gwilim and see what he could learn, but the room was empty. Angwyn turned toward the stairs and they climbed to his chamber as the cough returned again. "We were well met. There are many alliances. It is complicated."

Ramonth chuckled. "Isn't it always?"

Angwyn lost his humor. His hand rested on his latch as he turned to stare at his captain. "Kinross."

"What of it?"

"Gone."

"Gone?" Ramonth's voice and brow rose.

Angwyn sighed as the images of the destruction and deaths returned vivid in his mind. "Declared a rebel stronghold by Governor de Warenne."

His captain shrugged. "Then we are better for it."

Angwyn pushed open his door. Were they? How was this different than when they defended Wales? "They are a brash bunch. I fear there will be repercussions."

Ramonth leaned a shoulder against the door fame as Angwyn stepped into the chamber. "Let them come. What chance do rag-tag degenerates have against English steel? Better we are rid of them all."

"You forget we were those 'rag-tag degenerates' but a few years ago." Why could he not see the similarities between their peoples? Was Ramonth so enamored of the English now that they were gifted this holding that he'd forgotten the cost of it?

His captain shrugged again and turned to leave. Apparently, it was only Angwyn's conscious that pricked him. He pushed his door closed with a huff. Why couldn't he step into the role as one of Edward's chosen few and embrace all he had been gifted? The English lords had been right. He hadn't fought to earn his place here. Why not enjoy it?

Isabelle tried to focus on the mending in her hands, but poorly suppressed giggles were causing her to poke her fingers more than the cloth. Water splashed behind her where Henric frantically scrubbed away what the lord had done to him. If that was the worst of his punishment, her brother had gotten off easy for all the trouble he'd caused. The last lord, or that foul guard Gandry, would have killed him.

Muther stomped from the chamber that was only separated from the rest of their hut with a tattered bit of cloth. She held Henric's soaked clothes in her hand.

Isabelle bit the inside of her check and kept her head down.

The door swung open and Da ducked under the lentil as he stepped inside.

"Ye!" Muther pointed at him.

Da stopped with the door only half closed behind him and tipped his head at his wife.

"This be what ye hev brought us to." Muther shook the wet clothes at him.

"What be ye yappin' aboot, woman?" Da closed the door and crossed his arms as he stared.

She waved the clothes at him again. "That *lord*. That disgustin', revoltin' despot of a—"

"What be ye yappin' aboot?" Da asked again.

"This." She thrust Henric's clothes into Da's hand and Isabelle bit down on her cheek a little harder. "That man. That—that despicable … He—" Muther stepped forward and whispered in Da's ear.

Da's lip curled when she stepped away. He glanced at the sopping clothes in his hand, and his vision narrowed for a moment.

Muther crossed her arms with a grunt. Maybe Isabelle should have been more appalled. It was gross but it could have been so much worse. Sure, the lord had disrespected her brother in the act, but it was better than dead.

Da sniffed at the clothes quickly and then more deeply. Then, he started to chuckle.

Isabelle glanced between him and Muther who stood with her mouth gapping open as Da's laughter grew to a roar.

Muther's fists set on her hips. That was never at good sign. "Ya think this be funny?"

Da held his stomach as he reached the clothes back to her. "Ya," was all he could mutter though his laughter.

"I keen what English piss smells like."

Da wiped at a tear. "'Tis wine, woman. White wine. Appears … thee lord … of the keep … has … has had his revenge." He said through his laughter.

Muther snatched the soiled clothes out of his hand and sniffed them herself. She glared at Da, chucked them on the floor, and whirled to the back room.

"Nay. Dinae tell him. He ain't been that clean in a month."

Isabelle poked her finger again as she looked up at Da and joined his laughter.

Chapter 24

Conwy, Wales

Gwendolyn stood at her window, staring out at the rays of light breaking through the clouds and sparkling off the Conwy River. Life in the castle with King Edward had been such an adventure. Sumptuous meals, fine clothes, and being part of the respected nobility had made her feel like a child because of the wonder of it all.

Her fingers caressed the necklace she'd been given by the king. It was lovely and worth more than anything Angwyn and she had had seen since before their downfall.

Angwyn filled her thoughts more each day. She wanted to know how he fared in far off Scotland. They'd received no word. She sighed, remembering Katlyn's warnings the day they'd gone to the market. Gwendolyn had been so cross with her maid, but in the following days she'd seen them ring true far too often.

She laid the necklace on the table and walked from her room with a brush over her fine linen gown. A small part of her would miss this, but she wanted to be with Angwyn.

Gwendolyn crossed the bailey and turned toward the inner ward where the king and his officials resided. After passing through the inner gate, she tapped on the door of Lord Amersham's antechamber.

"Come."

She stepped inside the well-furnished room with its large window that added light to several cushioned chairs, shelves of scrolls, and a large desk in the center where the lord sat.

At the moment, he wrote on a long piece of parchment. The man was a few years her senior, but his hair was thinning. He wore it long enough to brush his ears. Though she knew he'd fought with King Edward, his lean frame made her believe the man more suited to these administrative pursuits than hardened battle.

"Pardon, Lord Amersham."

He at last glanced up and offered her a smile. "Lady Gwendolyn, what a pleasure. How may I assist you?"

"I was wondering if there was any news."

"My lady, it is too soon." He used an indulgent tone with her as though he spoke to an impatient child. "Scotland is such a vile place. We will win out, but you must allow time for things to settle."

She bristled at his manner. Gwendolyn fought to keep her tone light. "Yes, but I did hope His Majesty might have received a report." Surely the king received word at least weekly of the state of affairs in his new land. He was the king, after all. Angwyn had been gone for two months now. The king had to have heard something in all that time.

"I am afraid the region of Din Osways is not a priority for the king at this time."

She blinked at him. Not a priority? "Then that is well. If it is not a priority it must be because it is at peace." She wanted to believe her words but what if it wasn't important for another reason? What if the king didn't care what happened to it—or to Angwyn and his men?

Lord Amersham set down his pen and stood. An indulgent smile spread on his lips as he rounded the desk to face her. "My lady, there is a large difference between *peace* and not *presently* at war. We will know soon enough."

She was truly tiring of this man treating her like a child. Her words were firmer this time. "I only desire to take my proper place at my husband's side."

The lord's condescending smile looked more like a sly smirk. "And who are we to judge what is proper? What is improper to one is opportunity to another."

Opportunity? The Lord God determined what was proper and that was to be with her husband. The man was trying to allude to something, but she couldn't see it clearly. "My lord?"

"Come now, my lady. I, too, have heard the talk, and have seen it with my own eyes."

Gwendolyn's heart pounded. "Lord Amersham, whatever you may have seen, I know nothing."

"Very well. But you should keep an open mind, Lady Gwendolyn. Think of the influence you can hold throughout the land if you should only choose to take it."

Gwendolyn stepped back, as her heart and Katlyn's warnings again thundering in her head. She didn't care at all for the way the man leered at her.

"You would make a most magnificent queen."

Gwendolyn gasped. "I am a married woman, Lord Amersham."

He shrugged. "For now."

Gwendolyn stomped forward two steps and slapped the man with a resounding crack. It echoed and stung her hand. "There is your *opportunity*, Lord Amersham." She whirled and stormed from his study.

The nerve of that man to think she would leave her husband.

She stormed back to her chamber and paced in the small space. "How dare that man presume such a thing. How dare he?" She glanced at Katlyn who stood wide-eyed on the opposite side of the chamber. "His Majesty has been nothing by courteous. He has shown me kindness, nothing more."

The maid shifted her weight between her feet and lowered her gaze.

Again, unease rattled Gwendolyn. "Is it not?" The truth was there, but she didn't want to see it.

"There are rumors, my lady," Katlyn whispered without looking up.

"What rumors?" Was this more of the noble Lady Bess' gossipmongering?

Katlyn looked at her and waved the rumors away, no doubt hoping to sooth her mistress. "None of them true, my lady. I assure you."

Gwendolyn's fist perched on her hips and she spoke slowly, enunciating each word. "What rumors?"

The maid sigh as her gaze dropped again. "That his Majesty ..." She took another deep breath and let it out in a huff. "That his Majesty finds you attractive. That you find him attractive."

Gwendolyn gasped, and had to steady herself against the wall. She dropped into a chair. "What have I done?" She'd been so enamored by the pageantry and the adventure. She'd put herself in a compromising position without realizing it.

Her stomach knotted and she pressed her hand to it. What if Amersham hadn't meant divorce. Her hand covered her mouth. Was it like King David sending Uriah to the heart of battle to assure he would be killed? Was she King Edward's Bathsheba? Her heart thundered in her ears. What if he was dead already?

She had never met the chancellor or the king before arriving at the castle after Angwyn left. Why try to pursue her, of all women? She was too old to bear him any children and, as a Welsh woman of minor nobility, she had no power to aid the king.

Gwendolyn's breaths came in quick pants. Nothing made sense. Was this a way to separate her from her husband to hurt him? She had to get word to Angwyn. But she couldn't send him a letter without being discovered and she had no way to travel to him without a proper escort and the king's leave. Gwendolyn shuddered. She'd struck the king's official, and refused whatever scheme they were concocting. What would they do to her now?

She was not a woman prone to tears, but she couldn't seem to stop them. She shouldn't have sent Gwilim with Angwyn. She could sorely use the former captain, even now wearing friar's robes, to aid her.

Amersham rubbed his cheek as he watched the Welsh lady leave. "I suppose I will have to alter my plans now." He released a huffed sigh. There were still many ways to play this. Governor de Warenne was due to return soon. Amersham would assure the governor did his bidding again—all the while thinking it was his own idea.

Amersham smirked. The powerful men around him were like clay in his skilled hands.

He returned to his desk and the paperwork he had to attend until his plans for the Kenseths were complete. Yes, there were still many avenues open for him to get what he wanted.

Chapter 25

Din Osways, Scotland

"Will ya hurry up?" Isabelle grumbled.

Henric dragged his toes in the soft dirt behind her. "I dinea keen why I hev ta go."

"Because Da said ya were to come."

"But I ain't a maid."

Isabelle whirled around to face him. If she couldn't get her bother to hurry up, the whole castle would be awake before they got in the gates. That couldn't be good. What would happen if she ran into Gandry or his men again? She shuddered and pinched Henric's ear as she bent down and glared at him. "Da said ya were to come and work for his lordship as a sign ya be sorry."

"But I ain't."

Isabelle pinched harder and pulled.

"Oiw!"

"Ya ought ta be. Ya keen how lucky ya be? Thee English can kill anyone of us for nay any reason—and ya've given them plenty. Now, hurry up." She jerked him forward as she turned and he freed himself from her grasp.

They climbed the steep ramp to the gate, slipped inside, and crossed to the hall. Pots clattered in the kitchen but there was no one in the hall yet.

Isabelle released a sigh and slowed her pace as she climbed the stairs to the lord's chambers. Henric's footsteps stomped behind her and echoed off the walls. She tapped on the door.

"Come in," Lord Kenseth called. He was dressed in what she thought of as his everyday clothes; a dark green sleeveless shirt over a tan shirt. He didn't have his armor on and his sword rested on the table.

He glanced up from a parchment he was unrolling on the table he stood next too. "You are early."

Henric peeked out from behind her and looked at the lord.

Lord Kenseth turned fully and crossed his arms. One brow rose high. "This changes things."

Isabelle pressed her hand against her knotting stomach. The lord had been kind—so far. But the English could turn cruel quickly. "Da sent him ta do penance."

Lord Kenseth held Henric in a hard stare and her brother gripped a handful of her skirt, pulling her collar tight against her throat. "Then we have come to an understanding, Henric? You'll not be attacking me or my men again?"

"Nay, sir."

"Good." He turned, secured his sword around his waist, and rolled up his parchment again. He smiled at Isabelle as he passed and ruffled Henric's hair. "This chamber could use a good scrubbing."

After a trip to fill a bucket, Isabelle set about making the bed, dusting the ash that seemed to coat everything, and straightening the chamber.

A splash of water hit the floor. Henric was on his hands and knees scrubbing the dark stones. "This be girl's work."

"Seems appropriate. After all, Da says ya throw like a girl." She chuckled as she turned back to her task. A wet brush hit her back which soaked the side of her dress. With the brush in her hand, she tossed it so it landed in the bucket, sloshing water over her brother's knees. "Aye, ya throw like a girl."

The sun stood almost over head as they crossed the yard again. "Hurry to Muther. She'll getcha somethin' to eat."

"Ain't ya comin'?"

"Nay, I'm supposed to help their priest with thee meals." She gave him a little shove toward the gates. None of the guards paid either of them any attention, as the guards were busy training and working.

Henric shrugged and continued.

Isabelle whirled around to head to the kitchen. A hand clamped over her mouth and an arm coiled around her waist so she couldn't breathe. Dragged backward, she was pulled into a room lined with narrow beds. With the hand still over her mouth, her captor slammed her back down on a table. Gandry loomed over her and her heart seized painfully. A dagger caught the light coming in from the only window in the room.

"You cost me, wench. Twice." He thrust the blade at her face.

Free of his arm around her, Isabelle threw out her arms, knocked his hand from her mouth, and jerked her head to the side. She wasn't fast enough, though and fire laced through the side of her ear where his dagger sliced her.

He grabbed the top of her dress. "Now, it's time you pay." His face hung close to hers and the rancid stench made her gag.

She thrust her hands against his chest and tried to push him away.

"I should kill you. But that would be a terrible waste, now, wouldn't it?" He thrust his hips forward, parting her knees and drew the flat of the dagger over her cheek.

Tears blurred her vision and fabric rent. She squirmed as she fought to keep his hands from her. Her nails caught on the back of his hand and he jerked away with a hiss. Freed from some of his weight, Isabelle reached for his face and dug her thumb into this eye.

Gandry roared and thrust the table away as he staggered back, holding his hand over his eye.

Isabelle rolled to the floor and scrambled under the nearest bed. It wasn't much wider than her but so low she had to slide on her stomach. She gulped air as she followed his stomping steps. He stood between her and the door. Her breaths came so fast and her heart pounded so loud she struggled to think clearly.

The bed over her vanished as it was overturned with a crash. Isabelle moved to under the next bed in the row, but it, too, crashed which revealed her. The rough floor scraped across her exposed skin where the vile man had torn her dress. Blood dripped on her hand from her ear.

Crash.

She fled to the next bed.

Crash.

He stomped on her skirt and she had to roll to break free and slide under the next bed.

Crash.

There were no more beds. Isabelle crawled to the wall and drew her knees up to her chest. Her lips quivered from her crying. Tears stung her eyes.

Gandry's dagger waved at her, his eyes narrow and hungry. He stocked step by pounding step toward her and licked his lips.

Isabelle couldn't do more than whimper. She had nowhere—

Bang!

The door slammed open behind the guard and Lord Kenseth stormed into the room. His captain was only a step behind. "You." He pointed at Gandry. "What is this?"

The sight of the lord angry at his own man only made her cry harder. Here, this Englishman had again come to save her.

"My lord." Gandry looked from Lord Kenseth to her and back

again. "She … she was stealing."

Isabelle closed her eyes and lowered her head as she clasped the pieces of her torn dress closed. How many times could this lord stand between her and his men? Surly he would believe her to be a thief over Gandry attacking her. She dared looked at the lord and pleaded silently with him to see the truth.

Lord Kinseth's hard gaze roved over the dagger in the soldier's hand. Then, it swept over her, seeming to take in her tattered garment and the blood sliding from the cut in her ear.

Gandry wiped her blood from his blade on the back of his leg and slid it in the sheath.

Had Lord Kenseth seen her blood on his blade? He'd been looking intently at her.

The lord's gaze returned to the guard. His jaw set with an anger that made her shudder. He took a pounding step toward the soldier and slammed his fist into Gandry's face. The vile guard crashed to the floor and his head bounced near her feet.

Henric squeezed in past the others, ran to her, and wrapped his arms around her neck.

She let him hold her as she relaxed against the wall. Isabelle met Lord Kenseth's gaze. With the anger still brewing on his face, there was something else. Sorrow? Regret? Sympathy? She wasn't sure. But of all the Englishmen she had ever met, she knew that she could trust this man. She feared his own men would turn against him for it, though.

ChapTER 26

Din Osways, Scotland

Angwyn's heart thudded as he stared down at another innocent who was bloodied and lying on the ground. He barely noticed Gandry groaning at his feet between two of his men. Oh, his rage made him hot. He pulled the collars of his surcoat and tunic from his neck to let in a little air.

"Are you insane?" Ramonth hissed in his ear as he turned his back on everyone else in the room.

Angwyn's gaze never left Isabelle's as she clutched her torn dress to herself. "It seemed like the appropriate response at the time."

"You did it in front of that girl and the boy. Do you think they won't tell everyone in the village what they saw?"

Good. Let the word spread Lord Angwyn Kenseth would not tolerate vile behavior from anyone—not even a man under his command. Wouldn't that make his job easier? His vision blurred for a moment as a cough tickled his throat.

He turned his gaze to Ramonth at last. "The discipline of the men falls on you, captain. I consider this to be *your* failure, not mine. Do not let it happen again." He raised his chin to Hywel and Eudav. "Pick him up."

As Angwyn turned to leave the room, he glanced back on Isabelle. "Have Friar Gwilim look at your wound." He stood out of the way and waited for her and her brother to leave behind the soldiers. When she drew near, his fingers brushed her arm and she looked up. "Did he …?"

"Nay, m'lord. Thank ya"

He nodded as they passed through the door and looked to Ramonth. "Gather the men, captain."

Ramonth stared wide eyed at him with his jaw slack.

Angwyn again pulled at his collar. Did the platform sway? He cleared his throat of another cough and he looked down on the courtyard at the English guards lined up on his left and his soldiers on his right. Gandry stood restrained in the center between Hywel and Eudav.

He wiped his brow with the back of his hand and cleared his throat again. "By order of King Edward, Hammer of the Scots, we are charged with bringing order to this wretched land. As vile and repulsive as you may find your situation, you *will* do as we are commanded. Out of chaos we bring order. Out of order we will bring control. And from control comes dominion."

With a hand on the rail to steady himself, Angwyn suppressed another cough and moved to the stairs. They swayed in his vision for a moment before he stepped down and stood in front of Gandry. "One does not gain dominion by inciting chaos itself." His gaze shifted from the glaring man to look at his soldiers. "We are soldiers of the king, here to bring law to a lawless land." His hard stare tuned to the guards. "How you have behaved in the past—is the past. Law will reign this day." He turned his stare back to Gandry. "Those who disagree will pay for their actions."

Gandry spit in Angwyn's face. An odd rumble bubbled around him. His soldiers were incensed at the action and the guards seemed ready to join the mutiny.

Angwyn wiped his face with his sleeve and turned to Ramonth. "Strip him."

Gandry gasped and jerked to free himself of the two soldiers. "Nay."

The captain took a moment before he moved. He gave a quick nod at last and stepped forward with his dagger drawn. Renting fabric filled the silence as Ramonth cut the Din Osways' coat of arms from Gandry's garment. The yellow shield was divided diagonally by a blue band with three yellow diamond shapes. Above the stripe in the right corner were two boar heads. Under the stripe in the bottom left corner was a single boar head. By striping him of the crest, Gandry had no standing in the army. No one claimed him. He was set adrift to fend for himself without rank or anyone to guard him in a fight.

Angwyn's gaze swept over the guards and blurred slightly as he again pulled at his collars. "You may have had your own way under Lord Sintest. Lord Sintest is dead! And so are his ways." He turned to look at all the men and a wave of dizziness almost made him close his eyes. He fixed his stare on one point on the wall and cleared his throat yet again. "We are here to build a *better* Scotland. Any man who disobeys my orders, any man who acts in a manner contrary to our edict from the king, will incur my wrath."

He glanced over his shoulder to Ramonth, and regretted it. "Remove him."

Hywel and Eudav followed the captain as they pulled Gandry toward the gate. The disgraced guard dug in his heels and jerked in their grasp to stop their forward movement. In a few paces, Gandry was shoved out of the gate and onto the steep ramp outside. Angwyn's soldiers formed a line to stop Gandry from returning.

Angwyn turned his attention back to the guards and fought the dizziness that came with the movement. "If anyone else wishes to test their skills outside these walls, there is the gate." He pointed as he coughed. "No matter how vile and uncourted these Scots may be, we are English." His heart stumbled at identifying as anything by Welsh. "We will not gain our God-given right of dominion over this land by acting in a way more vile than those we rule."

The men murmured, but no one dared answer.

With slow movement, Angwyn glanced again at Gandry. He still stood just outside the gate, glaring. He spat on the ramp and tightened his grip on the sword on his hip. Then, he squared his shoulders, turned, and stomped down the ramp out of sight.

Angwyn dismissed the men as he pulled at his collar again.

Ramonth followed him inside and down the hall to the meeting chamber. "You are playing a dangerous game."

"What would you have me do? If I allow them to act as animals, we are no better than this pagan rabble we have been sent to suppress." Angwyn reached for the wall as the hallway pitched.

"And what was that about my fail—"

Angwyn's knees buckled.

Chapter 27

Din Osways, Scotland

Gwilim returned to Isabelle and handed her a cowl. She quickly pulled it over her head. The wide collar covered the damage to her garment as he pushed back the hood and turned her face to look at her ear. The deep gash still bled. "You are a very brave lass."

As Gwilim pulled his bag of medicines into his lap he glanced at Henric, who clung to his sister's side. "And you too, young lad. Very brave to come back and find his lordship when you did." *Thank you, Lord.* He couldn't bear to think of what Gandry had intended to do to the lass.

Isabelle winced at his touch.

"My pardon. But we don't want the wound to get worse, do we?" She shook her head.

He examined the cut closely. It should probably have been stitched, but he had nothing to offer her for the pain. He smeared on some ointment that would help stop the bleeding and aid with healing.

"There now. Almost done." He wound a small cloth over it. "You are very blessed, child." He held Isabelle's gaze. "I do believe his lordship favors you."

She pulled back and her hand covered the place under the cowl where her dress was torn.

Gwilim smiled and patted her shoulder. "As a child of God, dear. He has no children of his own." Pain laced through him and his smile faded. "Not anymore, anyway."

The door opened and footsteps pounded toward him. Ramonth stopped at his side. "Your services are needed."

"Yes, one moment."

"Now, friar."

Isabelle took hold of the cloth he'd been wrapping around her wound and offered him a small nod.

Gwilim sighed, stood, and turned to follow.

"You'll need those," Ramonth said as he point to the medicines Gwilim was placing on the table.

He secured the bag and hurried after the captain. Gwilim hadn't crossed the room before he saw Isabelle and Henric leave hand-in-hand. Her mother would no doubt be able to finish what he'd started.

They climbed the keep steps and Gwilim followed Ramonth into Lord Kenseth's chambers. The lord was in bed. His raspy breaths filled the room.

Gwilim pushed past the captain and hurried to the bedside. He didn't need to put a hand on the lord's red, sweat-dotted brow to know the man suffered. "He is feverish."

"I am fine. I just need rest." Lord Kenseth's cough said otherwise.

"Rest, yes. Fine, no." Gwilim turned to Ramonth. "I will make an elixir with what I have. I will give you a list of what else I need. I have never seen anything like this. It came on so quickly."

Lord Kenseth grabbed his arm. "No one can know."

"Pardon?" Why ever not?"

"No one." Kenseth sputtered again.

Ramonth sighed. "We are at a very fragile time, Brother Gwilim." It must have been bad if the captain had referred to him so formally. "His lordship cannot be known to have any weakness."

Gwilim glanced between the two men. "Surely, someone will notice his absence."

Ramonth shook his head. "As far as all are concerned, Lord Kenseth is planning our defense. He has left me in charge of the daily operations, and you are the only one allowed in here, besides me."

"You want me to lie?" Gwilim crossed his arms.

Ramonth widened his stance. "Who else would you be allowing in?"

Gwilim's arms dropped to his sides. "No one. He needs his rest."

"Then, it's not lying, is it?" Ramonth said.

Gwilim huffed. He moved to the table and made a list of the things he would need on a scrap of parchment before he handed to the captain. When the man left, he pulled a small pot from beside the hearth and started to make the elixir. The room soon filled with the strong scent of herbs as the medicine warmed over the flames. It would need to cook for just a bit and then cool enough to drink.

Gwilim sighed as he watched the flames dance. The meal would be late. Isabelle would be no help to him and, now, he had the added weight of his ailing lord. What would become of him if he failed to save the father, as he had the son? *Lord, I need Your help.*

Muther had her change her dress as she sent for Da. He'd come home quickly. Isabelle had tried not to cry as she told him how the guard had attacked her.

"I turned, and her were gone, Da," Henric said. "She'd been right there, then her weren't. I heard her cry. There were a practice sword on the ground I coulda used, but I went to get the lord."

"He came crashin' in and punched his man, Da. Laid him out flat," Isabelle gripped her father's arm.

Henric stood with his feet apart and his arms crossed. "Heard them others say when we we're leavin' the lord done throwed him out."

Da sighed. His eyes were sad. "Ya hev done well to tell me. For now, off to bed. I need time ta think."

Isabelle watched the way Muther stared at Da as she followed her brother to their beds. She hadn't stopped shaking all the way home. She wrapped her thin blanket around her and curled on her side. Her ear throbbed in time with her thumping heart.

Chapter 28

Din Osways, Scotland

Gwilim stretched his arms. Light streamed in bright and cheery, but Lord Kenseth lay unaware in the bed. He drew the cool damp cloth over the lord's face, neck, and collarbone, but it did little to quell the man's fever.

Dipping the cloth back in the basin, Gwilim rung it and brushed it over Lord Kinseth's skin again. He was not a trained healer. He knew the fundamentals of cleaning wounds, and basic elixirs, but whatever the lord suffered from was beyond his skill. Again, his impending failure caused his fear to grow. He closed his eyes against such an awful fate. A long sigh slipped out of him as he dampened Lord Kenseth's skin again. "He must get well." It was more of a plea and prayer than directed at the captain who stood clean and rested on the opposite side of the bed.

"Go get some rest, friar. You've done all you can do." Though Ramonth's words were kind in tone, they still spoke of Gwilim's failure. Ramonth didn't believe any more could be done either and that Lord Kenseth would die.

"It is never all. But I am afraid it is in the Lord's hands now. My knowledge in this matter is not enough." Just like his skill with the sword hadn't been enough. Gwilim would never overcome his many failings.

The captain walked around the bed and placed a hand on Gwilim's shoulder. Though he'd intended it to be a kindness, the weight of the man's hand seemed only another impossible burden to carry. "Go rest, my friend. If your God is there, He has already heard your prayers."

Gwilim lumbered to his feet and hobbled to the chamber door. He glanced back at Lord Kenseth as he pulled open the door. He brushed his brow with his sleeve, lowered his arm, and opened his eyes. Isabelle stood outside the lord's chamber. Gwilim drew back with a small intake of air. He'd almost run into her. "Oh, dear."

The girl's gaze shifted from Gwilim to the chamber. As the lord's bed was opposite the door, she no doubt had seen the situation.

Gwilim stepped out, shooing her back as he moved, and closed the door behind him. "His lordship will not be needing any cleaning today."

Isabelle's mouth opened.

Gwilim turned her and urged her down the hall to the stairs. "Come along. You can help me prepare the meal."

He led her to the kitchen, pulled out a stool, and tapped it for her to sit. She complied as he picked up a large basket of potatoes and set it beside her. Then, he brought a large bowl of water and small brush. Picking up one of the tubers, he dipped it in the water and scrubbed off the dirt, demonstrating what he wanted her to do.

Isabelle smirked and rolled her eyes as she took the brush from him and grabbed another potato.

She was not a child and Gwilim should have known better, but he was not himself after tending to the lord all night.

They worked quietly side by side, Isabelle cleaning and him peeling. She stole glances around the room. Her gaze lingered on the various food items around them. The door swung open and a servant dropped another basket of potatoes beside her. Isabelle groaned quietly.

It would be best if he distracted her. "Now, Gwilim is a name dating back to the Roman days. Of course, my parents were not Roman. I guess they just liked the name. Is Isabelle a traditional Gaelic name?" He smiled as he popped a slice of tuber in his mouth.

"'Tis French."

Gwilim paused, the raw potato still on his tongue. "French?" He finished his bite. "Now, why would a good Gaelic mum and dad give their daughter a name from France?"

The girl lowered her gaze and her hands rested in the water with another potato. "'Cause they were French."

"Were?" Gwilim could not do anything right. He'd meant for a lighthearted bit of conversation with the lass and it was clear he'd upset her.

She focused on the potato in her hands and scrubbed.

Gwilim placed his hand over hers to still them. "Child?"

She handed the potato to him and met his gaze with a teary one. "Me parents came here. They passed from an illness. York and Ellen took me in. Them provide as they can."

"God's peace be upon you, child. And His blessing to York and Ellen. It is good of them to care for you."

She nodded and as she reached for another potato. Her eyes again strayed to all the food around them.

He'd seen it in the village. These people had nothing. Here, he nibbled on the potatoes she cleaned, surrounded by all the food they had in abundance, while she had nothing. Gwilim slid from his stool and picked up the basket they'd emptied already. He waved for her to follow. "Come, child." They walked to the larger store room and he swung the door open.

Isabelle gasped at all the food crammed inside.

"You are a child of God. And you shall live as one." Gwilim pulled fruits and vegetables off the shelves and put them in the basket on his arm. Next, he added small bags of grain, and a larger one of flour. "This isn't much, but you are welcome to it. Now, this is not charity." He knew the Scots to be a proud people. His trade in the village of the keep's surplus had not gone as well as he'd hope because of it. "When you are not helping his lordship, you will help me in here. As long as you are able to do that, his lordship will have no question as to how you are recompensed." She had to grip the heavy basket with both hands. "Now, have you eaten today?"

She shook her head.

"Come." He led her back to the table, pulled a bowl from the stack, and filled it with stew from the pot he'd left to simmer over the low flames in the hearth late last night as Ramonth had tended Lord Kenseth. He pushed aside the bowl of water and brush, and sat the stew on the table. He patted the stool again and turned to fetch a spoon.

Isabelle had the bowl to her lips, sipping the contents before he returned.

Chapter 29

Din Osways, Scotland

Odd smells tickled her nose as Isabelle climbed out of a light sleep. She blinked at the large stone hearth with its glowing coals near the corner where she lay. Where was she? She tuned at a small *thunk*. The castle kitchen. The priest had brought her here earlier. She helped him clean potatoes.

Isabelle rolled over and sat up on her elbows, watching the big man grind something in a mortar. Herbs by the smell of them. Her empty bowl from the stew he'd given her sat beside him. The basket heaped with goods was near her. Muther would be happy for the gift of her wages. It would help feed them all.

Gwilim poured the herbs he'd ground into a small cloth and gathered the corners, twisting it to make a sealed pouch. He set the round bulb of it in a cup and poured steaming water over it slowly. He held the pouch of herbs in the water for a few moments before he drew it out and squeezed the excess water out of it into the cup.

He gathered the cup in his hands and his gaze met hers. "I need to take this to his lordship. I will be back directly."

After he left, Isabelle stood and crossed to where he'd worked. She sniffed at the herbs and shook her head. If the lord was sick, this wasn't going to make him better. She glanced around the room and spotted the ingredient she needed. After all that Lord Kenseth had done for her and Henric, the least she could do was help him get better. The remedy was simple and she was surprised the priest hadn't made it.

She cleaned the bowl she eaten her stew from, added a good portion of mustard powder and an equal amount of flour, and slowly tipped added hot water from the kettle Gwilim had used as she stirred. When it was a thick gooey paste, she took it up the stairs to the lord's chamber. The sharp scent of the mustard played in her nose as she climbed.

"I'm afraid he is getting worse," Gwilim said as she raised her hand to knock on the door.

Another, much deeper voice floated through the closed door. "For all our sakes, I hope you are very wrong."

She knocked softly, not wanting to disturb the lord.

"Go away!" came a loud shout from the other man.

She knocked again, and this time the pounding of angry steps came toward her. The door flew open and the lord's captain glared at her. "You?" His scowl deepened. "Lord Kenseth does not need any or your *services* today."

His words were low and harsh, but his insinuation that the lord ever treated her shamefully was worse. She staggered back a step and held up the bowl with the mustard plaster.

"Isabelle?" Gwilim appeared beside the captain and pushed him out of the way. "How dare you." He glared at the captain. The priest must not have liked what he had implied about her, either. Gwilim turned back to her with a smile. "What is it, child?"

She reached out the bowl to him.

The captain wrinkled his nose and his lips twisted in disgust. "Dear God." He waved his hand in front of his face then pointed over her head. "Out!"

Gwilim lowered the captain's arm. "Wait."

"For his illness," she said quietly as she watched the captain.

Gwilim took the bowl but shrank from the strong smell as well. He glanced up from the bowl and stared at her with his brows pinched tight together. "You … you can't expect him to swallow this."

Isabelle covered her giggle with her hand as she dared another glance at the stern captain who stood beside the priest with his arms crossed. She shook her head. These men really didn't know what they were doing. She didn't trust herself not to laugh so she rubbed her hand over her dress from her throat to below her collar bone. "'Twill heal," she managed to stammer.

"How do we know this isn't poison?" The captain continued to glare at her. How could he believe she'd do anything to hurt the man who had saved her—twice?

Gwilim carried the bowl to the sick lord. His lordship really did look awful. "Then, she wouldn't have brought it herself." The priest opened the lord's shirt and began to smear the paste on his chest. The captain's glare remained on her until he closed the door.

She had done all she could. Isabelle turned and descended back down the stairs. She crossed to the kitchen and retrieved the basket of food the priest had given her.

The courtyard was busy. A few men glanced at her but they quickly returned to their work. With Gandry gone, she walked with her head up and stepped out of the gate. Her feet padded over the long ramp and she made her way home.

"I were paid for me work today," Isabelle said as she stepped inside the hut Ellen and York shared with her.

Ellen turned from her mending. "Them English parted with some coin?"

"Nay." She held up the basket.

Ellen came and inspected it. "Well, 'tis better than naught." She glanced up and held Isabelle in a long stare. With a gentle finger, Muther tucked some loose hair behind her injured ear. "I suppose it be thee least ya deserve for all ya endured, lass." She cradled Isabelle's cheek for a moment. "I wish it could be more."

Isabelle couldn't hope for more. She'd already been taken in by strangers, and saved from a horrible fate by the lord. They gave her a job, treated her well, and fed her. In this life, that was more than many had.

ChApter 30

Din Osways, Scotland

Ramonth stalked though the courtyard and watched the guards and their soldiers train. Sintest's men were an undisciplined lot. "Arms up. Block the attack."

A guard recoiled as his arm was struck with a wooden practice sword by his partner.

"If that had been a real blade, you would have lost your arm. Pay attention, man." Ramonth passed these men and proceeded on to the next.

A soldier thrust at his opponent and the other man leapt out of the way.

"On the battlefield you won't have the room to dodge a pike stabbed at your gut." Ramonth groaned, slung a shield on his arm, and waved the attacking soldier to repeat the action at him. As the wooden sword jabbed at his middle, Ramonth brought the shield up under the man's sword arm and shoved it away. Before the soldier could reposition his weapon, Ramonth delivered a mock lunge of his own to the soldier's stomach.

Ramonth waved the guard who had failed back into the practice combat. "Do it again."

With a tip of his neck, Ramonth tried to release some of the tension plaguing him. Lord Kenseth was in bed with some grave illness. He wiggled his nose, remembering the pungent treatment the girl had brought. If he were a praying man—

"Won't even face us, the coward. His almighty lordship knows banishing Gandry was a foolish action. And over that strumpet." Orion had his back to Ramonth and hadn't seen him approach.

Ramonth seized the back of his shirt and jerked. "Mind your tongue, unless you would like to be next."

Orion narrowed his gaze. "If he ain't a coward, where is the lord?"

"I told you, he prepares for the coming battles. No easy task when his choices are taking his best fighting men to assure victory, means leaving the rabble behind to tear down his keep. Or taking the rabble and dying because they refuse to train properly." Ramonth shoved the man away and released him to stumble several steps. "Drinking and assaulting women is the only thing you lot are good at."

Alistair caught his friend and they both turned to glare. "The only reason the lord threw Gandry out was to have the tart for himself."

"That will be enough of that talk." Ramonth raised his voice loud enough for all to hear. He had thought otherwise too. But Gwilim had been insistent as he applied the stinking paste the girl had brought that the lord's relations with the girl were honorable.

Orion snorted. "There's a wedding planned in the village. I'm sure his lordship will take advantage of the Prima Nocta." He raised his brows, testing Ramonth's response.

Several chuckled around them.

"And when he doesn't, what will you do then?" Ramonth didn't know what Kenseth would do with the distasteful practice. It was expected by the English, but even Ramonth couldn't stomach the thought of taking another man's bride on her wedding night.

He turned to the others. "Back to your training. There's still an hour before dinner. And if the talk against Lord Kenseth doesn't end, you'll take the last two watches on the wall for the next week."

The men resumed their mock battle and Ramonth continued to monitor, correct, and worry. These men would be entirely his responsibility until Kenseth recovered—and recover he must.

Ramonth trudged up the steps after dinner. He'd refused to unlock another barrel and the men had grumbled. He inched open Kenseth's door. The lord lay still in his bed, but as he approached, he noted the candlelight did not glisten on any sweat. The lord's breaths came deep and even with no sound of rasp or rattle. Isabelle's smelly paste seemed to have worked.

Gwilim slept in a chair, his feet propped up on a chest.

Ramonth gave Gwilim a nod. "May your prayers be answered in full, friar," he whispered. He was glad at least someone was praying.

Gwilim shifted slightly but didn't wake and Ramonth left the two men to sleep.

o⟩————⟨o

It had been three days, but Angwyn was out of bed and dressed today. The sun shone brightly through his window and touched the edge of the papers he studied. His captain had provided a list of the men he thought best trained and disciplined, another of those who would be good soldiers with some more training, and a final list of a handful of Sintest's men who Ramonth thought it best if they went the way of Gandry. But there would be a price to pay for every man he striped and banished.

Knock, knock.

"Come." The single word stirred the lingering cough. The latch clicked open and a gentle movement said someone stepped inside.

The name of the men Ramonth held in concern were those who had followed Gandry. Could there be a way to turn them into proper soldiers or where they too far gone?

Whoever had entered cleared their throat.

Angwyn glance over his shoulder to see Isabelle. Her hands were clasped in front of her. She didn't move to start her cleaning but gazed at him from hooded eyes. "Yes, what is it?"

"I … I wished ta thank ya, m'lord. For savin' me from that man."

Angwyn turned more in his chair and rested his arm on the back to look at the young girl more directly. "Brother Gwilim tells me I have you to thank for saving me. Some would say we are even."

She shrugged. "Aye, m'lord."

"I don't see it that way."

Isabelle's brows scrunched together and her head tipped.

"I am lord of this keep and this land."

She nodded. "Aye, m'lord."

"Some would say what I did was no more than my duty. This point can be debated as well, for only I know my own true reasoning. But you …" He smiled at her. "You had no duty. Some would even say it would have been to your benefit to not help me at all."

"It would nay hev been right, m'lord. To keen of a need and do naught about 'tis thee worst of thee darkness there be."

"You have done me a great service. One that shall not be without reward."

Isabelle's head came up a little higher and her brows rose.

"You, and your brother, have shown me there is hope in this land. You shall both, from this day forward, have my protection. As much as I am able, you shall be safeguarded by my very blade. My prayer and my vow is that you shall one day live without fear in this very land."

Isabelle dipped in a small curtsy. "Many blessin's m'lord. Yar kindness shall brin' peace to both our peoples."

"One day, may that be true. But I am afraid this day there is much fighting yet to come. As hard as we may hope, history has shown that kindness does not win battles."

The maid considered him for a moment and tipped her head to the side again. She offered him a single nod. "Nay, m'lord. But sometimes it has been known to prevent them."

Angwyn returned her smile. She was a smart girl.

She curtsied and turned "Gwilim wants me in thee kitchen. I shall clean in here later."

"Very good." The door clicked closed and Angwyn turned his attention back to the lists before him. If all these men were just more like that girl, his task would be so much easier.

Chapter 31

Conwy, Wales

Amersham crossed the bailey to return from the hall back to his study. Gwendolyn had been absent again. She'd given excuses of various illnesses but it was clear to him she wanted to avoid Edward.

He sighed. Matters would have been so much easier with her willing participation, but a mere woman would not stand in his way.

A disheveled soldier stomped to the castle gate. He was filthy and his surcoat tattered. No doubt another from the Scottish holdings. He was either a deserter seeking the king's absolution, or a man whose regiment had been attacked come to report the incident to Edward. Either way, Amersham paused to listen in order to better plan the best move for his betterment.

"Who goes there?" The guard at the gate held the new comer in his gaze as his pike angled across his path.

"Gandry, late of Lord Sintest of Din Osways. I would speak to the king."

"You will speak with me first, soldier." Amersham waved him forward and the guard allowed him to pass. The man smelled as bad as he looked. "I am Lord Walter Amersham, the king's chancellor." He glanced at the surcoat and noted that the damage to the fabric had been to cut the crest away. Had this Gandry fellow left Kenseth's rule, or had he been expelled? Amersham resisted a smile. Either way, this man could be very useful to him. "You have traveled far these few days. Tell me, why is a sergeant of the guard of Din Osways not with his men?"

Gandry spit on the ground. "Din Osways could go to hell."

Indeed, this man was just the fellow he needed. Amersham turned them toward the rear of the castle to talk with the man further. "How is it you came to be here?"

"That fool stripped me of my honor and threw me out. I found a few peasants and forced them to feed me and carry me part of the way, but it has still taken over a week to get here to the king. That man will pay for all he has done." Gandry's gaze bore into Amersham's. "That ingrate Welshman has no right to rule in the king's name."

"You speak of Lord Kenseth, I assume."

Gandry looked about to spit again but thought better of it. "I would gladly ride with a group of English, and kill that prudist Welsh myself. Then, I have a certain lass from that stinking village who will pay as well."

"But you are speaking of a lord, duly appointed by his majesty himself."

"That man is no lord. A village rat threw mud in his face and he wouldn't allow us to punish the brat or any of the villagers. Sintest had let us take girls as we had needed, in order to appease our desires and keep his men under control. Kenseth," he spit the man's name, "won't allow any of them to be touched."

"The men have needs," Amersham said, goading the sergeant's ire to a white-hot rage.

"As punishment for taking girls we didn't even get to enjoy, he had us labor on the keep. Manual labor that the villagers should have been forced to do."

Kenseth was making this too easy for him. "Is that so?" he asked.

"Aye, my lord. And if we weren't making repairs, we were training."

Well, that was understandable, all men needed training in preparation for the battle, but Amersham didn't say so.

"He allowed us only our meals, no other rest. I have served on night watch more times since that blackguard arrived than in all the time under Sintest. And—" Gandry jerked to a stop. "He locked away all the alcohol. We weren't allowed a drop—until he left for Scone and Captain Ramonth unlocked a *single* barrel for us each night."

Amersham rubbed his chin. "So, there is disagreement between Lord Kenseth and his captain?"

"Aye, Ramonth is loyal to the king and will fight these rebels."

Amersham nodded. "You have done well, Captain."

"Sargent, your lordship."

"You have done the kingdom a great service. And the king. If not captain, let us settle on lieutenant, then. A man of your loyalty should be rewarded." Amersham turned to a narrow path that led to his study. "You should meet Lady Gwendolyn while you are here. If what you have told me is true, she may still become your queen after all," Amersham said with a smile he couldn't contain.

The two entered the administration building and then his study. There was much still to do and Gandry was just the man to aid him.

ChAptER 32

Conwy, Wales

Gwendolyn descended the stairs with a sigh. In the last week since she'd slapped Lord Amersham, she'd tried to be on her best behavior and keep her distance from the king. She was running out of excuses not to dine beside His Majesty at the royal table. She hadn't seen Katlyn all day to send her regrets for this evening. How long did it take to deliver the laundry, anyway? Surely the girl didn't take to scrubbing the garments herself.

"My lady." Katlyn burst from the shadows as though she came from the inner ward and crossed toward her.

"Katlyn, there you are—"

"Quickly, my lady, you must return to your chambers."

"Katlyn, what has gotten into you?" The laundry basket with their clothes in it looked the same as when the maid had left hours ago. It perched on Katlyn's hip. "Why isn't the—"

The maid seized ahold of her forearm, as she cast a fervent gaze around the bailey. "My lady, I really must insist you return to your chambers at once."

Gwendolyn's own heartrate increased as she watched the vein in her maid's neck pound a furious beat. "What is the matter?" she whispered.

"Not here, my lady."

A couple walked across the open bailey on their way to the hall. Gwendolyn smiled as she acknowledged them. Once they were out of sight, she turned and lead Katlyn back to their chambers.

The latch clicked in place, locking them inside. The basket crashed to the floor and Katlyn leaned back against the door with her hands covering her face.

"Katlyn what has happened?" Gwendolyn couldn't decide if she should have scolded the woman or thanked her from saving her another meal with all eyes on her and the amorous king.

"'Tis terrible, my lady," Katlyn whimpered.

Gwendolyn's heart stuttered and she lowered to the chair. "Is it Angwyn—Lord Kenseth? Is he dead?"

Katlyn tossed her head. "Not yet, my lady."

"Not yet. What does that mean?" She took a deep breath to calm herself as much as to reassure her maid. "Come, Katlyn. Tell me what you know."

The girl staggered to a stool, plopped down, and fiddled with the hem of her sleeve. Her head shook side to side, and when she at last looked up, her eyes were puffy and her cheeks wet. "I was on my way to deliver the laundry when I saw a soldier stomp into the bailey."

"One of Lord Kenseth's men?"

Katlyn shook her head. "I have never seen him. He wore no crest. It had been torn from his surcoat. He said his name was Gandry and he'd come from Din Osways."

Gwendolyn covered her gasp with her hand and slid to the edge of her seat. "Did he have word of Lord Kenseth?"

"Lord Amersham called him over and the two talked. Gandry had nothing kind to say of Lord Kenseth …" Her words dissolved into tears. After Katlyn alluded to some of the vile things the man had said about Angwyn, she continued. "I followed them to see what else I could learn.

Most don't notice a maid scurrying about doing her mistresses duties."

"Where did they go?"

"Toward the inner ward."

"Oh, Katlyn, that was too dangerous."

"I know, but my lady has been so eager for some word. You haven't found a way to tell Lord Kenseth what little we know. I thought I could ease your mind or gather more details to pass on to his lordship." Katlyn's trembling grew more violent.

Gwendolyn stood, offered Katlyn her hand, and they sat together on the side of the bed. She patted the maid's hand. "Tell me everything, then we will decide what is best to do."

Katlyn told of all the terrible things the soldier had said and done and how Angwyn had tried to stop him. He was protecting the Scots under his care from this Gandry fellow. Her heart fluttered and ached at the same time. His kindness for those Amersham and Gandry wanted destroyed would be Angwyn's downfall. They'd use it against him. But she was proud of him.

Gwendolyn patted the maid's hand again. "Very true, Katlyn. Lord Kenseth is a man of mercy and justice. If he removed this Gandry, it was for good reason. Is that all you heard?"

Katlyn's tears started again as she shook her head vigorously. "The sergeant told Amersham all about the defenses of Din Osways. He betrayed Lord Kenseth."

Gwendolyn tried to swallow the lump strangling her. It sounded as though he had set Angwyn up to be attacked. Her mind rattled at the possibility. "What did Lord Amersham have to say to this information? Does he plan an attack against Lord Kenseth?"

"He thanked him and raised his rank." Katlyn gripped Gwendolyn's hand tighter and glanced up with a pained look in her watery eyes. "Rewarded, my lady. The man is going to be rewarded for turning against Lord Kenseth." Katlyn took the kerchief Gwendolyn offered and dabbed her eyes. "They moved inside the inner courtyard where I couldn't follow."

Gwendolyn stood and turned to pace across the chamber that seemed to get smaller with each day.

"The last I heard was Lord Amersham laugh. 'There is great wealth held by these Welsh ingrates.'"

Gwendolyn dropped into her chair again. The king wanted to use her as a hammer to bring her people into line. And Amersham hoped to kill Angwyn to make her marriage possible for him to steal all their lands. "I have been such a fool," she muttered as she fell back in the chair. "How could I not see this?" She closed her eyes and listened to Katlyn sniffle. The first night, when Edward had called her to sit next to him, she had had her fears. She felt something was not right about his attention. But she'd let herself be swayed by pretty words, attention, new gowns, and shiny bobbles.

Sitting up straight, ideas flashed across Gwendolyn's thoughts. "We have to warn my husband." She couldn't let Angwyn die for her stupidity. She'd been a child playing dress up in a world where men were cut down for greed and lust.

Katlyn's breath stuttered as she tried to stop her tears. "With whom would we send the message? Who could we trust?"

"We …" Gwendolyn stood, took both of Katlyn's hands, and pulled her to her feet. "*We* must go. *We* must tell him ourselves."

"My lady?" The maid tried to pull from her grasp.

"Please, dear Katlyn, find me a way. You know as well as I do that my actions have been played as well. If for no other reason than we would be there instead of here—out of their grasps. Find me a way tonight."

With a straightened back, squared shoulders, and dry tears, Katlyn took to her duty. "Yes, my lady. As our Lord God does guide us, I will do all I can."

Gwendolyn released her and they each set about preparing for the departure. Fear ticked up her heartrate, but no more so than the thought of seeing her beloved Angwyn again. With God's favor, she could be with him in a fortnight. The thought sent her to her knees in prayer. If their escape was going to succeed, it would only be with the Lord's help.

Chapter 33

Din Osways, Scotland

Angwyn glanced out the window as a servant left his chamber with the tray from his breakfast. He drew in an easy deep breath. The Lord had seen fit to spare him and return him to full health, but he still had not rejoined much of the activity of the keep. Now, he was mired in a web of his own thoughts.

He could see activity in the village in the distance. He'd heard about the pending wedding that was finally to take place today.

Angwyn's hand rested on the keepsake box holding the bouquet of his love's affection. A smile tugged at his lips remembering Gwendolyn on their wedding day. Their lives had held such promise then. Now, they lived hundreds of leagues apart.

"The wedding is to be this afternoon."

Angwyn glanced over his shoulder to find Gwilim standing in his doorway. He turned back to gaze out the window. He couldn't make out much detail at this distance, but there was definitely increased activity. "So I see." With a deep sigh, the concerns plaguing Angwyn surfaced. "We must find a way, Gwilim."

"My lord?"

He couldn't face the man—even now. "I have never said this before, but you fought well *that* day." Angwyn almost choked on the pain filling him again. "I saw your situation far too late." If he had only noticed sooner … "All these years I have been angry. Angry at life. Angry at God. Angry at you, for no other reason than because you survived and my son did not."

With a fortifying breath, Angwyn turned to look at the friar—his former captain—directly. "And here today the cycle repeats. We are now the invaders, uninvited into *this* land."

Gwilim nodded slowly for a moment. "Unfortunately, my lord, even in this our past still haunts us." They stared at one another for a prolonged moment. "You are aware the men will expect you to invoke Prima Nocta."

Angwyn sighed and rolled his eyes. "There is no law demanding this first night debauchery. Our God cannot bless that which violates His will … It is only rumor spread to keep the peasants in their place."

"Not here, my lord. The villagers fear it. The men expect it."

"Sintest's men, you mean. They are a lecherous lot, as Isabelle can attest." Angwyn groaned.

"From what I have heard, the right of the first night has been practiced against these people, my lord."

"Edward has never spoken of it. The lords I met with in Scone never talked about Prima Nocta. It is an evil rumor." Angwyn wanted to believe his words were true. He needed it to be the reality in this small part of the world he ruled. He turned away from the friar and closed his eyes. If he ignored it, the village would celebrate, but the authority over the men under his command would be swept away. Those men, in turn, would revolt against him. If he acted on it, it would violate his own wedding vows, anger God, and further enflame the Scots against any English rule. "Yet, it is my charge to keep the peace," he muttered.

"By your own words, my lord, one does not achieve dominion by creating chaos."

Was there any way to avoid it, in this situation? Angwyn glanced out the window again at the village as he nodded. Whoever thought it right to take another man's bride on her wedding night was vile beyond all reason. He could not cave to the men's lusts. Nor could he put aside his own vows to Gwendolyn so easily, nor violate God's will so profoundly.

A tap sounded on his door and he waved a servant in. The man handed him a missive and departed.

Angwyn took a moment to read it. What was the governor thinking? This had to be the worst battle plan ever conceived. How had the English ever defeated the Welsh with plans like this?

"Trouble, my lord?" Gwilim asked.

"There seems to be no end to it." He glanced out the window at the growing festivities. One problem at a time.

Angwyn turned and stalked to the door. "Pigs," he mumbled as Gwilim stared at him with a scrunched face.

Conwy, Wales

Gwendolyn gasped as Katlyn burst in the door.

The maid kept her gaze on the ground. "I tried to find a way to get us out of here, my lady, but I was sent away from the castle stables."

Fear rattled her insides until Gwendolyn trembled like a hapless damsel. She closed her eyes and drew in a deep breath only to release it slowly. The Lord did not give her a spirit of fear. Why couldn't she concoct a way of escape? "Oh, Katlyn. We have to find a way to get out of here. I cannot be part of what these men are scheming and we must get word to Lord Kenseth." Gwendolyn turned and paced the small space in the center of her chamber. Nothing came immediately to mind. "Will you pray with me, Katlyn?"

"Of course, my lady."

They knelt beside her bed and prayed long after the sun had set.

When God did not present them an answer, they went to bed, but Gwendolyn couldn't sleep as she tossed and turned. It was the wee hours of the morning but she didn't hear Katlyn's soft snores either. "Are you asleep?" she whispered.

"No, my lady."

"Can you get into the laundry?"

Katlyn's voice pitched with her confusion as she spoke from the dark. "Yes, my lady. They see me there often."

Gwendolyn sat up in bed and lit the candle on the table beside her as the idea bloomed in her thoughts. "Good. I need you to collect a few things. Does the housekeeper from our estate, Hunydd, still make trips to the market?"

"I saw her there last week, my lady."

Gwendolyn held Katlyn's wide-eyed stare. Her heart quickened as her fear evaporated into excitement. "The Lord God prepares the way for us, Katlyn. This is market day, and we need a few things. You should be there when it opens and it would be good that you should *happen* upon Hunydd, for we need to get word to our people. We need their help."

The maid now sat up with her feet over the side of her bed. "What are you going to do, my lady?"

"I am going to meet with Lord Amersham and request a boon."

Katlyn jerked to her feet. "My lady." The maid's hands pressed to her chest. "The man is dangerous."

"That he is, but our God is greater. Have faith, Katlyn."

Gwendolyn listed the items she wanted. They spent the time until the sun rose, putting special, personal belongings in one of Gwendolyn's trunks and talked through the plan.

The late summer sun shone brightly through the window as Katlyn left to complete her tasks.

Gwendolyn placed the necklace King Edward had gifted her around her neck and smoothed one of her fine gowns as she considered her reflection in the mirror. This would help her convince Lord Amersham of her intentions and attest that the men still had sway over her.

Before she left, she knelt beside her bed again. "Lord, I trust in Your guiding hand. Protect us and give us favor. Go before us and make our path smooth."

She stood, brushed her hand over her gown once more, and left. With God's favor, they would leave by midday.

Gwendolyn pushed back her shoulders and raised her chin as she approached the inner gate, only to see Lord Amersham exiting toward her. He wore a thick cloak, and carried a small satchel. "Good day, my lord."

He jerked to a stop and stared at her. "My lady. We haven't seen much of you of late."

"You gave me much to think about in our last conversation, my lord." She kept an easy smile on her lips and tried not to think of how this man was plotting to kill her husband.

The sunlight caught on her necklace and Amersham's gaze dropped to it. He smiled. "I see."

"I have a boon, my lord."

"It will have to wait until I return. I must see to some important business for the king, my lady."

Gwendolyn's heart pounded. No doubt that business had to do with Angwyn. She needed something only Amersham could grant her. He would be the key to saving her husband or losing him. She turned and followed him.

Chapter 34

Conwy, Wales

Gwendolyn scurried to keep pace beside Lord Amersham as he brushed her need aside to rush about his dreadful business. "My request should not take but a moment, my lord." They neared the stables and she smiled. "I wished to borrow a small cart to carry my maid and me home to Llwyn Gwyon."

Amersham jerked to a stop and his gaze narrowed. "And why might you be wanting to go back to the Kenseth estate, Lady Gwendolyn?"

She smiled and tipped her head innocently. "Well, you see, my lord, you and the king have been so very generous to me. I now have so many lovely gowns and gifts, I have quite run out of space in my chamber. I wish to take a trunk of my old things back to the estate to get them out of the way. I also wish to gather a report of His Majesty's harvest on our lands this summer, so I might share the news with him at supper. It will be a quick trip."

He considered her for a long moment before he resumed striding toward the stables. He greeted the marshal and instructed him to prepare a cart with a driver for her. "There you are, my lady." He inclined his head as he accepted the reins of his horse. "I look forward to seeing you when I return in a few days."

She lowered in a curtsy. "Good day to you, my lord."

"The cart will be ready in an hour, my lady," the marshal said.

"Very good, sir. My maid and I will be ready."

Gwendolyn laid the necklace gifted from the king on the dressing table near the silver hairbrush and fine comb. These items had no appeal anymore and she saw them for what they were—distracting shiny bobbles. She glanced around the room for any personal items she couldn't bear to leave behind. Finding none, she turned and descended the stairs to join Katlyn.

So far, their plans were proceeding smoothly. The driver, Thomas, was a man with a military bearing. His dark hair was trimmed very close to his head, but his brown eyes were kind. He helped Gwendolyn into the seat as Katlyn sat on the back end of the small cart with her legs dangling over. The trunk she was returning to Llwyn Gwyon sat between them.

The small cart tipped as Thomas climbed onto the seat beside her. He picked up the slender strips of leather, snapped them gently against the tan horse's back, and clicked his tongue. The cart ambled slowly through the castle gate and into the town. Thomas turned them to a side street to avoid the crowd still in the market who would notice her departure.

Gwendolyn sent a silent praise to her good God. He had indeed prepared the way for them. Yet, she struggled to sit still as they plodded along slower than she could walk.

Thomas nodded to the guards at the city gate. "Where am I taking you, my lady?"

"Llwyn Gwyon, my estate." She pointed to the road leading away from the castle on their left. "It sits about half an hour away, there on the rise."

Thomas encouraged the horse to a quicker pace but it still was not fast enough to suit Gwendolyn. She glanced back twice to see if anyone followed them, but she only saw men and women returning from market either with their purchases or empty containers after they'd sold all their goods for the day.

She wore the same gown as the day she'd arrived at the castle. To stop her fidgeting, she smoothed the rough fabric over her knees and clasped her hands. They had this one opportunity to get away from the manipulations of the king and Lord Amersham. If they didn't leave now, they may not get the chance before Amersham enacted his plan to kill Angwyn.

The cart entered the stone wall of Llwyn Gwyon. Her home. She loved it here. The rows of small leafy pants said they would have a good harvest of potatoes this year. She didn't think she'd get to enjoy any of them. Her eyes swept over the estate. This was likely the last time she'd see it, for fear of what Lord Amersham would do to her and Angwyn.

Thomas drew the cart to a stop between the house and the stables. Several servants stopped their activity and looked up curiously.

"My lady?" A maid gasped. Several others nearby turned with open mouths and wide eyes.

Gwendolyn's hands gripped tightly together. Katlyn said she had spoken to the housekeeper. Yet no one looked as though they expected her.

"Welcome home, my lady," Hunydd said as she stepped from the house. "We did not know you would be returning today."

Gwendolyn managed a smile as Katlyn hopped down. Of course, they shouldn't have known she was returning. Hunydd gave no signs she knew either and Gwendolyn wondered, as the female servants stood about staring, if the housekeeper had told anyone else. "It is only a quick visit, Hunydd. I needed to return a few things to the house."

"Of course, my lady. We just finished our meal."

"Wonderful." Gwendolyn took Thomas' hand as he helped her down. "I'm afraid I stole Thomas before he had a chance to eat."

"And I'm starving," Katlyn said.

Hunydd glanced at the man. "You can follow me." Hunydd held Gwendolyn's gaze and nodded.

The man was barely out of sight before a young groom darted out of the stables leading a horse that pulled a slightly larger wagon. The back held a blanket with hay spread it out over the it. A large bag Gwendolyn assumed was food for the journey sat in the front corner. They added her trunk she brought from the castle to another that probably held garments for them both.

"Come, my lady." Katlyn waved her to the nearest door, the home of the groom and his parents. She and Katlyn changed quickly. Katlyn now wore rough men's garments, and Gwendolyn donned a course kirtle.

Katlyn folded their gowns and added a couple more things they would need once they arrived in Din Osways to take to the trunk in the wagon.

Gwendolyn took only what she would need for travel. Most of it would be left behind. There was nothing that could be done about it.

Katlyn pushed her hair into a knit cap and wrapped a heavy wool cloak about her shoulders. She ushered Gwendolyn to the wagon. The maid helped her up, and covered her in the blanket and the straw. They thought it best for her to hide as they left Wales. Few would take note of a lad when the search for a noble woman and her lady's maid began.

She didn't know what Hunydd had in store for Thomas, but hopefully it would be hours before he tried to return. At that point, he was to be told to go back alone and the women would return in the morning.

The wagon tipped as Katlyn climbed to the seat, then the wagon lurched forward. It rumbled over the hard packed grounds and away from Llwyn Gwyon. The movement battered Gwendolyn's body, but it was her soul most troubled. Would they reach Angwyn in time? Would she ever see Llwyn Gwyon again? *Please, Lord, continue to give us favor.*

The wagon rumbled forward. Katlyn didn't say anything and Gwendolyn tightened the blanket around her to keep out the cold of the approaching night and to cushion her against the battering of the wagon boards. It was not a dignified or comfortable way to travel, but if they could escape and get to Angwyn without being discovered, it would all be worth it.

She drew in a deep breath. *Thank You, Lord, for getting us this far. I trust in Your goodness to see us to our destination's end and to protect Angwyn.* She released the breath and settled in. Sleep quickly claimed her after the previous night of little sleep. It was a long night, at peace at last.

Chapter 35

Din Osways, Scotland

Laughter and music greeted Angwyn and the men who followed with him to the village. They were all here, his men and the villagers. Ribbons twirled in the air as the village celebrated and danced around the couple. Again, thoughts of his own wedding and the following celebration blurred his view of the party before him.

The rhythmic tapping of the small drum, the jingle of the tympaun, and the singing fumbled and fell silent. All eyes took in Angwyn and his men who spread out around the crowd. The only sound remaining was the low rumble of the wagon Gwilim led into the village square.

The friar had been right. These people were terrified. They backed away from his men, and the groom took a step in front of his bride, shielding her from view.

Angwyn sought a friendly face among the eager lecherous gazes of the guards and the fear of the people. He spotted Isabelle. She stood tall and looked at him without fear. Henric stood beside her, his head tipped to the side watching. But Isabelle's gaze never wavered.

With her trust fortifying him, Angwyn turned back to the crowd. "People of Din Osways, you have heard it said that King Edward has made a declaration."

The guards smirked and nodded. If he did this, there was nothing stopping them from taking any of the young girls in the village. "As lord over the village and land of Din Osways, upon the marriage of any local inhabitants, it is said I have the right to Prima Nocta."

"No!" The groom shielded his bride more closely behind his back. He almost stumbled into her when one of his men punched him.

"Hold!" Angwyn shouted as he pointed to his soldier. Even his own men thought they had a right to abuse these people. "Hold your ground."

Don't insight chaos—in either group, Angwyn reminded himself. He turned to the groom with his pointing finger. "And your tongue."

Angwyn dismounted and stood in the center of the circle. "I have the right of Prima Nocta, the first night, with any and all brides from any village or land under my rule." Just saying the words of this lie turned his stomach.

No one moved around him. The village men stood in wide stances with their arms rigid at their sides and hands fisted. His soldiers' gaze swept the crowd with their hands on their blades. The guards surveyed the women and practically drooled.

Angwyn waved Gwilim forward.

The friar approached with a bundle held tightly in his hands and cradled to his chest.

"As lord of Din Osways, it is said I have the right of Prima Nocta. But a right is *not* an obligation." He let his gaze sweep from the couple, to the villagers, to the guards. "You have been taught since the days of the Romans, 'Therefore a man shall leave his father and mother and hold fast to his wife, and they shall become one flesh.' Marriage is a sacred vow, a binding contract recognized in all the realm. King Edward himself would not refute this."

Again, he looked to the guards. His next words rang through the still quiet space. "By declaration this day, before all gathered here and as God is my witness, I today relinquish my right to Prima Nocta."

"What?" Ramonth's sharp bark came before the rumble of the guards as they narrowed their gaze on him.

Angwyn raised his hand to stop Ramonth. "Hold your tongue, captain."

The guards bent their heads toward one another. Their grumbled words were so muddled they couldn't be understood. They glared and tightened the grip on their sword hilts as their attention turned from the maidens to him.

Angwyn stepped toward the couple with Gwilim at his side. Orion and Alistair, the two guard who come with Gandry to offer him a maid, moved to block their path. The two guards had their swords half drawn from their sheaths.

Angwyn squared his shoulders. "Stand. Aside."

His men shifted as though they meant to leap to his defense at the slightest twitch. The air turned stagnate as Alistair glanced at Orion, the soldiers, and Angwyn.

Angwyn shifted his weight to continue forward and at last the two guards homed their weapons and stepped away. The heat of their rage was almost as tangible as the lingering fear on the couple he approached.

Gwilim held the bundle still with one hand and unwrapped it with the other to reveal a piglet. Seeing the large crowd, the animal kicked and squirmed in the friar's large hands.

Angwyn took the piglet from him and, as he passed her to the bride, it squealed and thrashed. Though he'd only meant to speak to the couple, he had to raise his voice to be heard over the little piglet's cries. "To your new life."

The bride and groom glanced at one another and back at him. At last, the bride reached for the squirming piglet and cradled it in her arms.

"May it be abundant for the benefit of all." He inclined his head to the couple and turned to see the village thane, York, and his wife Ellen.

Angwyn stepped aside to speak to the man.

York spoke first. The big man bobbed his head in respect. "Thank ya, m'lord."

"You have the friar to thank, and your daughter. The vow of a man and wife should be respected here, just as it is in England."

York gave a sharp nod of his ascent and raised his chin. "Aye, Lord Kenseth."

Angwyn glanced around. It was worse than Gwilim had reported. "You have no feast for the couple?"

York kept his tone level and did not accuse. "We hev very meager amounts."

Angwyn pointed. "In the friar's wagon, you will find what you need."

Ellen dipped in a curtsy. "Thank ya, m'lord. Thank ya." She waved to several other women nearby and they moved to unload the wagon.

York offered him a nod and Angwyn returned to his horse. After he settled in the saddle, he found Isabelle in the crowd again. She smiled at him as she moved to join her mother and the other women.

As he turned his mount to return to the keep, Orion, Alistair, and several other guards turned their hate-filled gaze from the women they were denied by him. Angwyn sighed. He'd done right in the eyes of the Lord. He'd kept his own marriage vows. Isabelle had been proud of him. But the trouble with the men under his command had grown worse for all the good that he had done. There would be trouble in the days ahead.

Chapter 36

Din Osways, Scotland

The din in the hall caused the ache in Ramonth's head to turn to a relentless pounding.

"He refused his right as lord over them and made us look like fools!" Orion shouted with his fist in the air. The guards who had served under Lord Sintest were in a rage.

"He chastised me before he did that defiant Scot!" That came from Kenseth's own man, Cyaran. He'd punched the groom for refusing his bride to Lord Kenseth. Thankfully, he was one of only a few of the Welsh soldiers who sided with the irate guards.

"He coddles these people—"

"—and gives them gifts!"

"Enough!" Ramonth bellowed over the shouting and pounded on the head table.

Only a few quieted. Orion was not one of them. "We won't have it!" The guards answered his shout with something close to a battle cry.

Ramonth held the defiant guard in a hard gaze. "Curb your tongue, or I will cut it out myself."

A few of the guards lowered to sit on the benches around the tables —but not enough.

This was all Kenseth's fault. In truth, Ramonth sided with many of these men. The lord had acted rashly and undermined their authority with the people they were charged with ruling. But he had to maintain order or Ramonth would fail in his duty to the man he swore an oath to.

He drew in a deep breath and swept a slow gaze over the rabble. "Lord Kenseth is lord of this keep by law of his Majesty the king. *Every* man in this room *will* show respect due that position. And *every* man in this room will not forget their own position, or I will personally remind them." The next words caught in his throat. "Lord Kenseth made his choice."

"And shamed every man in this room in the process." Orion's arm swept out to include the men around him.

Ramonth agreed, but before he could counter the guard, the door swung open and Kenseth entered. Gwilim walked smugly beside him, a content smile on his face. He was at the root of this trouble. The friar and the God he served.

Kenseth was more sober. His sharp gaze surveyed the room and rightly judged the turmoil surrounding him. The lord squared his shoulders, raised his chin, and marched toward the front of the room. With his hand on the hilt of his weapon, most stepped aside and let him pass.

As Kenseth neared the front, Alistair remained steady and blocked his way.

Kenseth barely slowed until he came nose to nose with the man. Standing only a few inches taller, Kenseth glared down on the guard until he too stepped aside. Their gazes remained locked as the lord passed. He rounded the head table and stopped beside Ramonth. Looking out at the men as they glared back at him, Kenseth drew his sword. He held it out, pointing at them, but let it drop flat on the table with a deafening clatter in the silent, tension-filled room.

"There is my weapon. The blade that saw battle in Deheubarth,

North Powys, Snowdonia, and beyond. The blade that has protected life and has taken it. You stand here thirsting for blood. Well, there it is. Gaelic blood, Welsh blood, and English blood." Kenseth's words echoed until there was silence once more.

"You question why I choose as I do. There is your answer." He pointed at the blade. "I have seen battle since before some of you were old enough to hold a sword. I have tasted victory and I have known defeat. I know the difference and I know when a battle is won or lost." Again, he paused so his words might sink in.

The Welsh soldiers nodded their heads as their stances relaxed.

Kenseth turned his hard gaze on Orion, Alistair, and those standing rigid around them. "One thing I say to you today is I did not come to Din Osways to fight a war that was already *finished*." With his weight braced on his fists on the table, Kenseth directed his words to the guards. "As much as you detest the people of this land, the people of Din Osways are not your enemy, *unless* you make them so. You question my leadership and, thus, my authority. Where is my authority? Where is my power? Is it in this sword?" He straightened and swept his hand through the air over the weapon. "Am I any less powerful standing here before you with my sword on the table?"

It was a challenge. How many foolish decisions would Kenseth make in one day?

Orion was quick to take up the contest. He drew his weapon and lunged forward.

Kenseth snatched up his sword, put his boot on the edge of the table and shoved it into the charging guard.

Orion dropped back to the floor, and his sword skittered through the reeds.

Kenseth held the tip of his blade to the fallen man's throat.

Alistair was held back by another guard.

Welsh soldiers drew their blades and held the remaining guards in place. The air crackled.

"Hold your weapons," Ramonth ordered. It gulled him that he had to save Kenseth from the fallout of his own foolhardy actions. He stepped beside Kenseth with his hand on the hilt of his own weapon. "Any man here that dares to stand against the lord of this keep will taste my steel for his efforts."

"Stand down, captain."

"Any man!"

"Captain Ramonth! Stand down!" Kenseth now dared to put him in his place. His captain. The man who stood up for him before these men when he agreed with them. The man who was supposed to have authority over the men. Kenseth had undermined him in front of all of them. How was Ramonth to do his job now? He stepped back and stared as a small part of him hoped the guards would teach his old friend a lesson.

Kenseth focused on the guard lying at his feet and raised Orion's chin with his blade. "This man drew his weapon against *me*. As lord of this keep, I have the *right* to take his life for such an offense."

Was he talking to the men, or was the lord further chastising him? Ramonth crossed his arms.

Kenseth spoke to Orion. "You objected to me forfeiting my *right* when we were in the village. Do you feel the same now?" He pressed the tip of his sword into the soft flesh between the end of Orion's chin and his throat.

Orion sucked air in through his nose and stiffened.

Kenseth held for another heart beat before he withdrew the weapon. "Lucky for you, you are needed by the king."

The lord raised his gaze to the rest of the men. "You want blood instead of peace. Then you shall have it." He straightened and took a wide stance, his sword firmly in his grasp. "If you are lucky, it won't be your own. There will be no talk of mutiny. We have a war upon us. Now, disperse from this. We are English, and we shall act like it in *all* manners."

Kenseth waited for any to challenge him. "I am lord of this keep, and I will rule as *I* see fit for the benefit of the land in *my* charge. Now, you will prepare yourselves. We leave for Stirling in two days."

This time, he didn't wait for a response. Kenseth sheathed his weapon and stalked from the room. Alistair helped Orion to his feet as the rest of the swords were returned to hips and the men turned to leave.

Ramonth fisted his hands and stomped after his lord. Kenseth may have been done with the men, but he was not done with the lord. They would have words.

Chapter 37

Din Osways, Scotland

Kenseth's heart thumped in his ears as loud as his steps pounded down the hallway. An echo followed him.

"I saved your bloody neck." Ramonth came alongside him.

"I had the situation under control." He'd confronted Orion and the guards who were bent on evil. The trouble-making guard had ended up on floor with his neck on the tip of Angwyn's sword. He'd handled it.

"That was control?" Ramonth snorted.

Angwyn stopped to look at his captain more directly. "You usurped my authority in front of the men." His captain and friend had tried to control the men, suggesting he couldn't control them himself. Ramonth had ordered and threatened the men when Angwyn had been in the middle of addressing the budding revolt.

"I?" Ramonth's eyes opened wide as he sputtered. "Usurped?" He spit the word. "What the bloody hell do you call what you did in the village?" His gaze narrowed. "Every one of these men has spent years fighting against these blackguard Scots. And you turn around and give them gifts? What did you expect?"

"I expect to head off a rebellion *before* anyone else has to die." Why couldn't this man see? A little good would go so much further to turning the tide of the revolt than brute force. "'A soft answer turns away wrath,' the Scriptures say."

"Oh well, that's just fine. Let's go make nice to the rebels we are trying to suppress."

Angwyn leaned into his captain. "What I did, I did for the safety of the men *and* everyone under my rule. If you have issue with that—"

"I have issue with that." Ramonth crossed his arms.

Angwyn straightened and stared at him for a long moment. "There was a day, Inek, when you and I were of like mind."

"I used to think so. Today, you proved me wrong." Ramonth spun and stomped back the way they had come. Winning this land looked like it would cost him the friendship of a man he'd known from childhood. Angwyn sighed. It would be a steep cost, but it was for the good of so many. Isabelle and Henric came to mind. He did this for them and all the other children in Din Osways who deserved a childhood free of war.

Angwyn turned back to continue on his way. There were battles yet to come and they needed to prepare to leave for Stirling. He'd ask Gwilim to pray over Ramonth's heart.

Angwyn drew water from the basin in his chamber and rubbed his hands over his face. It had been a long afternoon. Between the fear of the villagers contrasted with the hunger of the guards, refusing to take part in the horrid farce of the first night Lord Sintest had apparently indulged in, to the near mutiny of the men, and the insult of and argument with Ramonth, he wished he could wash it all away. He regretted the kegs were still locked up. Not that ale ever solved any problems.

Knock, knock.

"Come." He turned expecting Ramonth to enter and set things right between them, or perhaps Gwilim to praise him.

Isabelle pushed open the door and stepped inside. She raised a brow.

"M'lord?"

"Yes, yes. Go ahead." Since his illness, she'd taken to preparing his room for the evening.

She moved first to the fire and knelt to stoke it to bright flames. Isabelle glanced over her shoulder at him. The light of the fire danced on her cheek. She was far too thin. "Me Da sends his thanks for thee gifts taday, m'lord."

Gifts. Simple food goods and one small pig. It wasn't much. While his men had hated him for it, the villagers were grateful. Would it be enough to win the peace with them? "My lord …" he mumbled.

Isabelle's head tipped to the side. "Pardon, m'lord?"

"What is a lord, child? Tell me."

"Ya are, m'lord. Ya are our authority, our leader."

Angwyn focused on her again. "A piece of parchment tells you this is so. But who is Lord over the lords?"

Isabelle sat back on her heels and nipped at her lower lip.

Angwyn waved is hand. "Speak freely, child."

"I hev only keen ya this short time, m'lord. But what I hev seen, ya are a good man. I believe in yar heart, ya keen what's right. The people, in the village, respect ya. Nay jus' for the sow, or the food. Ya gave them hope. Many … I, appreciate what ya hev done. Ya will be rewarded here and in heaven for the good ya do for yar people."

This child grew dearer to him every day. Her words had lifted his spirits. "It is a difficult thing at times to know who your people really are." It seemed he had more in common with Isabelle and her people than most of the men downstairs.

"Are they nay those who believe as ya? Those who respect ya for who ya are?"

Angwyn's gaze again lost focus as he nodded. "Thank you, Isabelle."

She offered him a wide, infectious grin as she stood and spun toward his bed. She turned down the bedcovers, and fluffed the pillow.

Those who believed as he did. The words rattled in his thoughts long after she left for the night.

Border of England and Scotland

The late afternoon sun peeked through the many white tuffs of clouds. Gwendolyn tossed the blanket off her shoulder and set up on one elbow. A long, rutted road stretched out behind them as the cart rumbled through a thin forest of alder, birch, elder, and even a few buckthorn.

She reached into the shrinking bag of supplies and drew out one of their last apples. She turned toward Katlyn perched on the wagon seat. "You have been driving for days with little rest."

"You cannot risk being seen, my lady."

"Then, we shall stop so you can rest." The poor maid hunched forward. "We are far enough away by now for a short rest, at least."

The jarring movement of the wagon stopped as Katlyn pulled back on the reigns and drew the horse to a stop. She sighed heavily. "Thank you, my lady."

Gwendolyn sat up fully and stared out at the trees beside them. "It is I who need to thank you. You have been truly loyal these many years." Even when Gwendolyn hadn't wanted to listen, Katlyn had been faithful to speak the truth.

"My lady, it is my pleasure to serve in whatever you need."

The truth of those words made tears pool in Gwendolyn's lids. Katlyn was a blessing in so many ways. She passed an apple to the dear woman and kept the last one for herself.

Gwendolyn's gaze swept over their surroundings. Her heart leapt into her throat and she stopped before she could take a bite. "Katlyn, how far have we traveled?"

The maid finished the bite in her mouth and wiped her chin with her sleeve. "Maybe forty leagues, my lady. Give or take."

Gwendolyn couldn't keep the tremor from her voice. "So, we are not in Scotland yet?"

"I don't think so, my lady." Katlyn shook her head slowly. "We should still be far from those lands."

"Then, who is he?"

Katlyn turned and her gaze followed Gwendolyn's finger to the smiling Scottish warrior in a deep yellow tunic standing with his feet apart in the middle of the road behind the cart. The maid gasped and moved to snatch up the reigns again when a full regiment of yellow-clad Scottish soldiers stepped out from behind the trees and surrounded them.

Gwendolyn couldn't breathe. She had put them in far greater danger than being caught by King Edward or Lord Amersham. Her heart pounded in her ears as she reached for Katlyn's hand. The maid grabbed it and held it tightly.

Chapter 38

Din Osways, Scotland

"Lord Kenseth." Ramonth marched into the meeting chamber as
Angwyn worked on the preparations for their deployment to Stirling the
next day.

The two men hadn't talked since Angwyn helped the village couple
celebrate their wedding. In the day between they'd both focused on their
tasks of readying the men. Angwyn looked up from the many
documents before him.

"There is a contingent of about a hundred English soldiers heading
this way."

Angwyn rose without a word and followed Ramonth to the
courtyard. His horse was already saddled, and a handful of his men were
mounted ready to ride with him.

As they cleared the gate and rode down the long ramp toward the
village, the arriving soldiers moved off the road and began to set up
camp in the tall grass.

Angwyn straightened in his saddle and approached the man garbed
as the commander.

The surcoat over the man's mail was dirty, and Angwyn believed
much of the stains were dried blood. The commander's long face was

pot-marked but clean-shaven, though his dark hair was made more so by the grease and grim coating it. The corner of the man's lips turned in a small smirk. "Ah, our welcoming committee has arrived."

Angwyn reined in his horse. "Well met, commander."

"Well met, Lord Kenseth." He gave a small incline of his head. "Pierson Fenwick, commander of His Majesty's men. You have done well here, my lord."

Good, the man recognized the order Angwyn had established. "We have kept the peace, if that is what you mean." That was the point of them being here, wasn't it? To stop the rebellions and rule in peace.

Fenwick continued to hold him in a hard stare. "I trust you will have room for me and my officers this night?"

"We will make accommodations." He didn't care for the commander's tone. He may have led a hundred soldiers, but Angwyn was a lord, and the man's superior.

Angwyn turned his horse and men back toward the keep. "I'll see preparations are made for supper and your stay."

The commander turned his attention to his men, and Angwyn returned to the keep. He found the friar in the kitchen. "Gwilim, we have Commander Fenwick and his officers joining us in the keep tonight. Prepare a meal and place for them to sleep."

"Yes, my lord."

The meeting chamber echoed with the slurping and chewing of rowdy men. Though only Fenwick and his three captains joined Angwyn and Ramonth, a person would have thought the commander's full force crowded the space for all the noise they made.

Fenwick leaned over his plate with his forearms on the table, and ate as though his food would escape at any moment. His fingers were drenched in the juices of the venison and boar Angwyn and his men had brought down in a hunt in preparations for their travels. The commander seized his tankard and downed several noisy gulps of ale. Much of it spilled from his mouth and added new stains to his shirt. He slammed the cup down and dragged his sleeve across his face before he attacked his meal afresh.

Gwilim and Angwyn exchanged glances.

Stomped steps drew Isabelle's attention.

"Get yar bruder, and hide, Isabelle," Muther said in a strained voice.

Isabelle stepped beside Muther and caught sight of soldiers as screams met her ears. "But—"

Muther gripped her shoulders and shook her. "These be nay Lord Kenseth's men, nor any man from thee keep. Run, child. Get Henric, an' hide."

Isabelle could barely breathe as she raced to grab her brother.

"Hey!" He tried to pull free.

Isabelle wrapped her arms around him as she pulled him down to sit in the shadows between her home and their neighbor's. "Shh." She held him tightly so he couldn't get away. Her pounding heart made hearing anything else difficult.

Angwyn thought he might have spared himself Fenwick's terrible table manners if he got the man distracted in conversation. "This plan is a curiosity to me. Stirling seems a poor choice on the surface."

The tactic didn't work because the commander kept eating as he answered. "Governor de Warenne laid out the plans himself." He stuffed a hunk of chicken in his mouth and continued. "His victories are many. I do not question his plans." He moved on to the creamed potatoes, scooping them up with his fingers to shovel them in his mouth. "Stirling sits in the center of this forsaken land." Fenwick licked his fingers, sloshed more ale in his mouth, and returned to the selection of meats. "Whoever controls Stirling can then control movement between the north and south of the kingdom."

The clamor of villagers struggling with soldiers leaked into the alley. Doors crashed, things were thrown around, bowls or jars broke. Isabelle couldn't tell who trembled more, her or Henric as they clung to one another.

"Nay, that be all thee bread we hev. Ya hev nay right to it!" Muther's strained voice brought tears to Isabelle's eyes. Ellen had used the last of the flour Gwilim had paid to Isabelle to make bread for the wedding. When Lord Kenseth provided the meal, they'd been able to save it for themselves. Now the soldiers were going to take it away.

"Right? It is your *duty* to provide for His Majesty's troops." The voice of the soldier was so cold that it made Isabelle shiver.

The terrifying metallic hiss of a sword being drawn made Isabelle's heart stop.

"Consider it your *privilege*," a different man said.

"And—" The commander shoved more food in his mouth. "The rebel Andrew Morey escaped from Chester Castle. Not long after he made his way back north and murdered the lord sheriff, Hesilig, then he gathered quite a few followers at the castle Avoch in Ross. He was prevented from taking Urquhart Castle, but it'd be best to cut down his rebellion again—and for good."

Angwyn tried to keep his gaze on his own, half-empty plate. "Again?"

"Aye. Moray and his father fought at Dunbar earlier this year. King Edward sent the elder Moray to the Tower of London, and the son to Chester, but the slimy snake escaped. It would have been better for us if we'd killed him."

Angwyn still struggled to grasp the point of the plan he'd been sent. "While I was at Scone, I overheard talk that de Warenne wants to reduce the number of soldiers at Stirling. Thinks they are too costly and the Scottish rebels can easily be put down with the forces we have."

Fenwick shook his head. "Governor de Warenne is making these battle plans first. He wants a quick end to matters. Then he can send some troops home." Fenwick raised his tankard high and Gwilim refilled it again.

"You forget, Commander, that I have been on both sides of that table." Angwyn had fought to stop Edward from bringing Wales under English rule. Now, he let that same king use him to help bring another country under his thumb. Edward had declared war on France now, too. When would the man have enough?

"That is right." Fenwick paused in his chewing and stared at him. "So, you must believe the Scots to be ignorant and brutish to be so stubborn against His Majesty's forces."

Did Angwyn think that? Had surrender brought his people any peace? Was oppression any better than resisting and war?

"Damn yar privilege and yar duty!" Muther yelled. Then, she gasped and let out a strangled whimper. Something clattered to the ground. The sound of something heavy falling met Isabelle and the low laughter of men filled her.

Chapter 39

Din Osways, Scotland

"Where's Lord Kenseth?" Henric whispered. "He said he'd protect us."

Isabelle wondered the same thing. The lord hadn't been in Din Osways long. There had been another before him. An evil man. Like those in her village now.

Da's roar startled her.

One of the invading soldiers staggered past the end of the lane where Isabelle hid in the dark. She covered Henric's eyes as the man dropped with an ax in his chest. Da yanked the blade free and charged out of sight. Men yelled. Women screamed. Children cried. Metal clanked against metal. They had pitchforks and axes. What could they do against English swords? Where was Lord Kenseth? Isabelle fought to silence her sobs.

<hr/>

Angwyn sat with Commander Fenwick and his officers. The man at last seemed to be concluding his meal. Angwyn was relieved he would no longer have to watch the Englishman eat while he talked.

Fenwick hefted his ale in the air. "You Welsh came to see the light. Because if you entertained any thought that these hillsmen are right, that would mean your people's surrender was made out of pure stupidity."

Gwilim stacked a pile of dirty plates and cups at one end of the table. He tensed at the commander's words. The mound of plates tipped and then happened to topple onto one of the commander's officers. Leftover ale splashed on his shirt, and food remnants fell in his lap.

Gwilim gasped and the officer growled.

"I am so sorry." Although Angwyn had the idea that Gwilim wasn't as sorry as he said.

The friar set down what was left of the stack and started collecting the dishes that had escaped and placed them back on the table. Then, he pulled a rag from his rope-belt and started sopping up the mess on the officer's clothes.

Angwyn had seen no other alternative than to surrender when he had fought king Edward. The battle at Dolwyddelan had been lost, their prince was dead, and so was Angwyn's son. But had he had more men, or any other option … Again, Angwyn found far more in common with the Scottish rebels than with the men before him. He understood their desire to be free men.

Angwyn sighed. Would Edward build castles across these green hills and subjugate these people until they were outsiders in their own land like he had in Wales? Angwyn did not wish that fate on anyone.

Fenwick pushed back from the table and stood. Angwyn, Ramonth, and the other officers followed.

Gwilim continued to mop up his mess from the man's clothes. "Pardon, sir. I do beg your pardon. Again, I am so terribly sorry."

The rest of the room stood, waiting.

The commander huffed; his narrow lips formed into a deep scowl. He gave a sharp nod to the soiled officer, who brushed Gwilim out of the way.

"Again, sir …" Gwilim stammered.

Fenwick cut him off as he turned to Angwyn. "Lord Kenseth. I thank you for the meal and the *entertainment.*" His words were dry and humorless. He led his men out and to their sleeping quarters for the night.

Angwyn was glad to see him go and dreaded the days of travel ahead with the man. He glanced at Ramonth who seemed at ease. Then, his gaze shifted to Gwilim. His brows were furrowed, making deep wrinkles form on his forehead, and his eyes were hooded. The friar slowly shook his head.

Angwyn agreed. Nothing good could come of joining these men. But what other choice did his oath to Kind Edward leave him? He stomped from the room and climbed the stairs. Nothing good would come of what de Warenne planned.

The chaos and shouts of the village grew quieter. Isabelle loosened her grip around Henric. "Stay here. Dinae be movin.' I'll hev a look and be right back."

She eased away from him and peeked out from between the houses. Muther's body was by the door of their home. A large bloody spot covered the gash in the front of her dress. The bread she'd tried to save lay scattered and trampled on the ground.

Not far away, Da lay on the ground and gasped one final breath. He was covered in blood.

The tip of a wooden sword appeared at her side. Henric raised it higher and lurched forward. Movement caught her eye and she picked her brother up, covered his mouth with one hand, and pulled him out of sight. As she disappeared around the corner at the back of the houses, she saw three soldiers pass the opening where they'd just been.

She crumbled on the ground with Henric in her arms and they clung to each other as they cried.

Chapter 40

Forest on the border

Gwendolyn trembled as more yellow-clad men joined those already surrounding their wagon. She'd been holding Katlyn's hand but the maid, jerked away, jumped down, and pulled a staff from the hay beside where Gwendolyn sat.

Katlyn gripped the simple weapon in both hands as she approached the large man behind the wagon who appeared to be the leader.

Chuckles met her bravery.

"You think I will not? Depart and leave us be." She swung the staff in the big man's direction.

He pushed the end of it away with a deeper laugh. "Put that away afore ya get hurt, lass."

"It is not I who will be hurting."

Gwendolyn admired her courage. She'd owe Katlyn more than her simple wage if the maid could get them out of this.

"By my God, you will not touch Lady Kenseth."

The laughter stopped, and a shudder raced through Gwendolyn.

"Lady Kenseth?" The leader's gaze swept from the maid to wash over Gwendolyn until she trembled.

Katlyn turned around with sorrow in her eyes. They both knew.

Katlyn shouldn't have said her name. But there was nothing to be done about it now. They were in the Lord's hands—as they always had been.

Din Osways, Scotland

Angwyn pulled his shirt over his head as a knock vibrated his door. It couldn't be Isabelle. He'd told the girl he'd be leaving today and she wouldn't need to see to the tidying of his chambers until later. Besides, she never knocked so commandingly. "Enter."

Ramonth stomped inside and Angwyn moved to a chair to pull on his boots. "Fenwick and his men are gone."

Angwyn glanced at the light coming from the window. "So early? I thought we would travel together."

"Appears as though they broke camp before first light."

"Why?"

"It may have something to do with the village."

Angwyn stood as his stomach soured. "What about the village?"

Ramonth released a long sigh. "Best if you come see for yourself."

Snatching up his sword, Angwyn pounded down the stairs. Like yesterday, his horse was saddled and ready. Gwilim stood nearby wringing his hands. The men—even Sintest's guards—were abnormally quiet.

Angwyn mounted and charged out of the gate.

He slowed as he neared the village. Broken pots, tattered clothes, and spilled food littered the ground. Doors were broken off their hinges. Small tables that had sat beside the doors were overturned.

He rounded the corner with Ramonth riding beside him. A handful of his soldiers and Gwilim followed on foot. Angwyn looked down into the tear-stained face of a woman leaning over her dead husband. The closer he got to the village center the more bodies he passed. The villagers who were still alive stood with hunched shoulders and glared at him.

He'd failed again. He'd failed to protect his own people. Here, as he dined with the commander, those under his care had been slaughtered. They had no weapons, they were peaceful, and had never given Angwyn a bit of trouble. Yet Fenwick's men had cut them down for no other reason than that they could.

His entire body shook, and a lump formed in his throat as he came to the village center. Where only two days ago there had been bright colors, merriment, laughter, dancing and singing—now there was death.

The bodies of two-dozen slain were laid out. The bride was one of them. Her new husband still cradled her lifeless body and rocked as he cried. York and Ellen were there too. She looked to have died of a single sword thrust, but York probably had taken some of the Englishmen with him.

Isabelle knelt over their mother. Henric over their father. She looked up at him with the same anguished stare he'd seen in Gwendolyn's eyes when he'd told her their son was dead. Isabelle had lost two sets of parents. It was too much for one young woman.

Henric snatched up the wooden sword lying beside his knee, popped to his feet, and charged at Angwyn's horse with a guttural roar.

Angwyn's mount reared. He gripped the saddle and tightened his knees against the animal, but he couldn't blame Henric. Angwyn's own heart had made the same sound when William had fallen.

Isabelle sprang to her feet, wrapped her arms around her brother and jerked him out of the way before the horse could harm him. She pulled him back to stand closer to their fallen parents.

The wooden sword waved in the air as Henric shouted. "Ya promised! On yar sword!"

Angwyn *had* promised. They were alive, but nothing would ever be the same for them. He'd failed them almost as badly as he'd failed

William.

"Me Da is dead 'cause of ya." Henrick's words were colored by his growing tears as he switched to Gaelic. "Chan e duine a th 'annad." Henric's tears grew to sobs. "Ya deserve to die," he cried. Henric spun and buried his face against his sister.

There wasn't much Angwyn could do now. "Bring these two to the keep," he muttered.

Ramonth rose in his saddle and swung his leg over his horse to dismount.

"Not you." Angwyn's words had been abrupt. The children didn't need a warrior—not now—not ever again. And Ramonth disagreed with his thoughts on how to handle these people.

Angwyn's gaze swept around them. The piglet he'd gifted the couple raced among the bodies with a squeal.

Gwilim straightened from offering last rites to a fallen man and glanced up at him.

"You," Angwyn said with a nod. The friar would be better. Isabelle knew him. He would be far gentler with the frightened children.

Gwilim nodded and inched toward them. He spoke softly in words Angwyn couldn't hear. The friar stepped beside them and waved them to walk in front of him. They passed Angwyn without looking up again.

Under the weight of the villager's hatred, Angwyn turned his horse and left. He'd offer to help bury their dead, but they'd never accept it. Everything he'd done in the months since he'd arrived had been thrust aside by a group of greedy, heartless men. How much longer could he champion their cause and the king who ruled them?

Chapter 41

Din Osways, Scotland

Angwyn slouched in his chair in the meeting room. His head throbbed in time with his aching heart.

Ramonth drummed his fingers on the table adding to the pain. "We can expect repercussions."

"They have nothing left," Angwyn said with a shake of his head. Too many of their men had lain dead in the village center. "I doubt they can even farm, let alone fight." He rubbed his hand over his face and muttered. "The village even smelled like death."

His captain sat tall and leaned forward. "Then, we must keep it that way."

He wanted the villagers dead? This was not the man he once knew.

"The rebel forces will get word of what has happened here." Ramonth thumped on the table. "I say surround the village. Keep the rebels out."

"Tell me, captain …" Gwilim stood in the doorway, his hard gaze narrowed on Ramonth. "When does it end?" His fist propped on his wide hips. "When do you decide you have won?"

"When they finally learn who is in charge."

"And who is in charge, captain? You? Him?" He pointed to Angwyn.

"King Edward?"

The friar was right. There was no order. This was not rule by law. This was anarchy and murder.

Gwilim snorted. "From the chaos we witnessed in the village, I would say there is no one in charge, no matter how much you wish it."

Ramonth sprang to his feet with such force his chair toppled with a crash. He drew his sword as he turned to face Gwilim. "How much *I* wish it?" He stalked toward the tall man. "What I wish is to restore order to our troops, and thereby this land. And to that end, I will not have you poisoning his lordship's mind with your frivolous twaddle." Ramonth raised his sword to point it at Gwilim's chest. "First the repairs on the keep, then the wedding, now what? Put us to work to rebuild that rat nest? They received what they deserved." The sword swung to the side at the end of the captain's rigid arm as it pointed. "Go back to your kitchen, friar. Do what you were sent here to do."

When Gwilim didn't move, Ramonth pressed the tip of his sword against the friar's chest.

Gwilim didn't flinch. "Very well. I will go. And I will do what I was sent here to do. And I will pray the Lord has mercy on your soul." He turned and stepped through the door but paused and glanced back. "In the end, my dear captain, the Lord God Jehovah will reign supreme, and you *will* need to answer to Him for how you treated His blessed people."

The friar left and Ramonth spun and homed his weapon as he stared at Angwyn.

Angwyn noted the hardness and rage in his former friend. "This wretched land now has us fighting our own." Ramonth opened his mouth, but Angwyn raised his hand. "Make your plans, captain. We leave for Stirling tomorrow."

Ramonth gave a curt nod as the corner of his mouth raised. "Yes, my lord." He turned and left.

Angwyn raked his hands over his face, trying to rub away the sight of the dead villagers. They would haunt him with the deaths of William and the warriors who had followed him into battle for Wales. Was there nowhere left within Edward's reach where there was peace?

Gwilim stomped down the corridor and across the hall. So many dead! People he'd tried desperately to befriend. They'd entertained and housed that commander while his men had—

He thrust open the kitchen door with a resounding bang. "Murder! They slaughtered those innocent people!"

He picked up the nearest bowl and hurled it against the wall.

"And that captain! Ramonth is becoming one of them."

A pot crashed against the stones of the hearth and clanged to the floor.

"I did not come here to be pushed aside!" He raised his fist to the ceiling. "Your Word is my command. But even David raised a sword against the evil in his land." He'd been a fool to ever set his aside. "I will not stand silent!" he roared as he heaved a jar of oil against the wall. It shattered and splashed its contents everywhere.

He stomped across the narrow room and jerked open the large storage room door. Isabelle knelt with her fingers laced together.

Gwilim staggered backward. Henric cowered in the corner. He braced his forearms on the table where he and Isabelle had worked only days ago. His head hung. "Dear Lord, forgive me."

He closed his eyes and slowed his breathing as he let go of his rage.

Swiping at a tear, he stood at last and turned back to the children. "Forgive me," he whispered. "I didn't mean to frighten you further." He waved them to him. "Come. I'll get you something to eat."

Isabelle stepped out of the storage room and reached for her brother's hand. He came to her side and wrapped his arms around her. "I dinae feel like eatin'," she mumbled.

"I know, child. You have seen evil no grown man should witness. I am sorry." He shook his head, unable to find the words that would bring comfort. "Still, you should eat a little."

He moved two stools to the table and the children sat while he prepared a simple meal for them. When he set bread in front of them, Isabelle wept. Gwilim could do nothing but hold her as she sobbed.

Gwilim had managed to get a little food in the children but they hadn't spoken. Isabelle now laid on a pile of empty flour and vegetable bags on one end of the storage room. He draped a blanket over her and forced a smile to his lips.

He turned and offered Henric another blanket as he stood behind his sister.

The boy snatched it out of his hand and stomped to a dark corner near a tall shelf.

Gwilim sighed. He'd hoped the boy would curl next to his sister so they could both be comforted. "Be brave, young lad. All will be well in the end." He had to trust God his words would be true. At the moment, even he struggled to see how God could bring any good out of this horrid situation.

He glanced again at Isabelle. "Are you comfortable enough?"

She nodded as she tucked the blanket under her chin.

"Keep him well," Gwilim said with a raise of his chin toward the boy lost in the shadows. "I will be just outside the door tonight."

She reached out and gently laid her hand on his arm. The weight of all her loss and pain seemed to be in that light touch. He patted her hand, praying with all his might that he could take it from her.

He lumbered to his feet, stepped out, and closed the door. He knew from his own experiences at Dolwyddelan, they would not sleep well tonight, or for many nights to come. He'd remain close, ready to leap to their side and assure them. It was all he could do.

Chapter 42

Din Osways, Scotland

Fenwick's arrival and his men's destruction of the village had delayed the men of Din Osways. Ramonth was ready to put a sword to any man so the rebellion would be over. Why couldn't Kenseth see it was the only way to restore order? Coddling angry men didn't bring about peace. Killing the troublemakers and keeping those remaining under strict rules was the only way.

He thrust open the barrack's door and found the men packing. Good. At least something was going—

"It's not right," Alistair grumbled. He had his back to Ramonth and hadn't notice the captain's entrance. "He's now even got those rat kids in the keep."

"Curb your tongue, and do your job." Ramonth left no room for argument in his order. Yet Alistair and his companion Orion had no discipline. They were a constant thorn in his side. The only reason Orion didn't lead the mutinous talk now was that he again served on guard duty on the wall. He'd been there frequently since his confrontation with Kenseth.

Alistair turned his scowling face toward his captain. "He is going to get us killed.

"He will save your neck, *if* you deserve it." Ramonth's ire grew each time he had to defend Kenseth when he, in fact, agreed more with these men. Angwyn had grown soft.

"You." Alistair point at Ramonth. "You I would follow in to battle. Not him."

The men around Alistair murmured their agreement. Ramonth would welcome the chance to lead. To take out these rebels and show them who was in charge. But for now, that was Kenseth, his longtime friend, and the man he'd sworn an oath of loyalty to.

Ramonth stepped toe to toe with Alistair and leaned in so their noses almost touched. His words ground through his tight jaw. "You are first and foremost a soldier of the king. You will do as you are told, when you are told, by whom you are told. This I will not waiver on. Am I clear?"

Alistair turned and everyone resumed their packing.

"We leave in an hour." Ramonth stomped from the barracks to finish his own preparations. The day was soon coming when his allegiances would be sorely tested. But for today, he was still Kenseth's man.

The door to the dark storage room creaked open, making Isabelle squint against the light.

"How are you two this morning?" Gwilim lacked his normal cheer, and she was glad for that.

Henric grunted. He'd cried much of the night. Isabelle not as much. York and Ellen were, after all, not her real parents. She knew the heartache of losing ones so close, and she had Henric this time. Before, she'd had no one and she had been younger than Henric.

She handed the blanket to Gwilim, took Henric's hand, and stepped into the bright kitchen lit with a fire and early sunlight through the window.

The big man waved his hand toward the table where two steaming bowls sat. "A bit of porridge to start the day. Then, Lord Kenseth has requested to see you both."

She nodded and slid on to the stool. The lumpy colorless mush did nothing to stir her appetite, but she sighed, and scooped a small spoonful into her mouth. The friar had sweetened it with something. She would have enjoyed it if …

She bumped Henric who sat with his elbows on the table and his chin on his fists. The lord had said he and his men would be leaving before … She didn't know now where their next meal would come from. "It's best if we eat," she whispered.

He only ate a couple bites, and she couldn't finish more than half. Isabelle took her brother's hand again and they left the kitchen, crossed the empty hall, and climbed the stairs.

Lord Kenseth called for them to enter at her soft knock. Their gazes met, he nodded, and waved them forward, but there was no smile on his face. He looked as sad as she felt.

He dipped his writing feather in a bottle of black liquid, tapped it on the edge of the tiny jar, and wrote something on the parchment in front of him. Isabelle didn't know how to read or write, and she watched with fascination as the feather wiggled and the tip made small scratching sounds.

"I have spoken to Brother Gwilim already." The lord glanced up at them, and his feather stilled. "It is not safe for you here."

Isabelle had been thinking the same thing. With the lord leaving and their parents dead, there was no one to stop the guards he left behind.

His kind, sad eyes closed for a moment before he looked at them again. "I can't undo what has been done."

She believed he would if he could.

"But I did make a vow—" His gaze met Henric's—"which I *will* uphold. I am sending you south. You will travel with the friar to Conwy."

Isabelle didn't know the place. It must have been very far away.

"My wife is there and will care for you both." He returned to scribbling as he continued. "Take this letter, and show it to anyone that gives you trouble along the way. It will give you safe passage throughout England."

Isabelle's heart hammered and Henric's hand jerked in hers. They were going to England? She didn't want to leave Scotland.

The lord put the feather down, corked the bottle, pinched a bit of what looked like sand, and sprinkled it over the parchment. After a moment, he folded it, melted the end of a red stick in a candle's flame and dripped a bit of it on the two edges to hold them closed. Then he pressed his big ring into it.

He looked up again and handed the letter to her. She took the other side, but he didn't release it. His words were soft as he stared into her eyes. "When this war is over and we can have peace in this land, I *will* send for all of you." He let go of the letter and sat back with a sigh that made his shoulders slump. "Now, go." He didn't sound like he wanted them to leave. "Brother Gwilim is already loading the wagon."

"Thank ya, m'lord. May thee Lord God protect ya." She meant it. This man had been good to her. She didn't blame him for what happened to York and Ellen. He would have stopped it if he could have.

He nodded as a small smile lifted the corner of his lips. "And you, dear child. Both of you." His words hugged her, but Henric sniffled, jerked his hand from hers, and raced out of the room.

She looked back at the lord for just a moment, praying she would see him again, and this place, and ran after her brother. *Please, Lord, let us come back.*

Chapter 43

Din Osways, Scotland

Isabelle raced down the stairs after Henric. They'd lost their parents, and now they were being sent away. She understood—she didn't like it—but she knew Lord Kenseth wanted them to be safe. They wouldn't be safe here without him and with the English killing people for no reason.

Henric wasn't in the hall, the kitchen, or the large storeroom where they'd slept last night.

She eased down the steps into the courtyard. The guards glared at her. Henric would have been too afraid to go near them.

Gwilim was loading bags in a wagon, but Henric didn't look to be anywhere around him. The gate was still closed, so he hadn't returned to the village or run off into the woods. Where could he have gone?

Remaining on this side of the courtyard, away from the men, Isabelle walked in front of the hall, and toward the back of the space where Gwilim was. If she couldn't find her brother by the time she reached the friar, he'd help her look.

Something moved in the shadow of a doorway. Henric.

She released a long breath and ambled over to him. She sat on her knees and held his tear-streaked face between her hands.

He scowled and tried to look unmoved, but his continued sniffling betrayed him. "I'll nay go."

"We must," she said softly.

"But this be our home."

Isabelle nodded as she let her thumbs rub his cheeks. "It was, an' will be again. But, for now, we must leave.

"Da would nay hev made us leave."

She pinched her lips together for a moment and closed her eyes. How did she make him understand? She opened her eyes and held his gaze. "Da was a brave man. An' so are ya. But sometimes, it be braver still to keen when we should nay fight. Now be the time to be safe until we can return." She raised an eyebrow and waited for him to respond.

Henric nodded a little, as she still cradled his face, and he sniffled.

"Promise me ya will n'ver forget this place. Promise me ya'll remember all of thee years we lived here, when thee rains were sweet and thee meadows green, so we can hev good years again."

Henric pulled from her hold, wiped his nose with his sleeve, and nodded. But his eyes quickly filled with tears again as he tipped forward, wrapped his arms around her neck, and continued to cry.

Isabelle held him tightly. She was scared too. But she trusted Lord Kenseth and Gwilim. If it was in their power, they'd make sure Henric and she returned one day.

Fists on his hips, Gwilim surveyed the wagon. He'd begun loading it by putting the supplies they'd need for the long journey in bags, but Lord Kenseth's words kept rattling in his head.

"I am entrusting these children into your care, Gwilim," the lord had said. Then, he'd laid a hand on Gwilim's shoulders and looked him in the eyes. "I trust you. The children aren't safe here. But in your care, when you deliver them to my dear wife, they *will* be safe."

With those words admonishing him, Gwilim had removed the supply bags and put everything in small crates. He stacked and arranged them so the children could crawl between them to a hollow he'd left behind the crates under his seat.

He gave his work a satisfied nod. Should trouble cross their path, the children would have a place to hide.

The men were in their formations ready to march out.

Gwilim scanned the courtyard, spotted the children across the way, and waved them over.

Isabelle kept her eyes on the guards nearest the wagons. She put Gwilim between her and them as she climbed into the back and sat near the crates.

Gwilim helped her brother up and Henric moved close to his sister. Both peaked under hooded eyes at the men.

Turning, Gwilim saw why. The hateful glares the men gave the children was enough to make him shudder. Had he not been standing there, or Lord Kenseth not been mounting his horse beside them, Gwilim had no doubt they would have tried to kill Isabelle and Henric. They were children, by all that was holy, what threat did orphans pose against armed soldiers?

Choosing not to provoke the men further, Gwilim inclined his head and did as the Lord God required. "Blessings on you. May the Lord keep you safe."

Orion spit on the ground at his feet. "There is your blessing, priest." He said the last word with disgust.

Alistair nodded and tapped his sword as though the lump of metal had some mystical powers. "My faith is in my blade."

Unmoved by the man's posturing, Gwilim raised his chin and held the fool in a hard stare. "Then, may the Lord protect your blade. And may you live long enough to learn the difference."

Mounted, Lord Kenseth moved to the front of the columns of close to eighty soldiers. "Men of Din Osways, today may we bring peace to all in this land once and for all." His gaze fell on the children for a moment before it shifted to Gwilim who nodded at him.

"I hope *all* don't mean his little Scottish friends." Orion said to Alistair with a snort. "There won't be none left when I get through."

A deep chill gripped Gwilim's heart and he shuddered.

A blade shot out and Orion stilled as it touched his throat. He raised his head until he looked at Captain Ramonth who held the blade. Ramonth snarled from the back of his horse. "You were saying?"

Lord Kenseth turned his mount and moved through the gate. Row by row the men began their march following him.

Gwilim watched until he couldn't see the lord any longer before he whispered a prayer. "Watch over Lord Kenseth protect him from both those before him in battle and those who would betray him from his back."

They waited until all the soldiers joining the battle were gone and the courtyard was silent. Hywel and a handful of Welsh soldiers had been left behind to guard the keep and what was left of the village.

Gwilim turned to the children. "We best be on our way as well. We have a long journey." He climbed up to the seat and clicked the horse into movement.

He slowed as they passed the village and allowed the children a long look—and prayed it would not be the last.

Chapter 44

Scotland heading to the English border

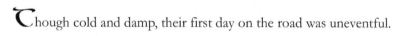

Though cold and damp, their first day on the road was uneventful. Gwilim glanced back at the children. They were so quiet that he found himself glancing at them often to assure they were still there.

Henric lay on his back, with his legs bent so his knees pointed to the sky, staring at the clouds floating by.

Isabelle met Gwilim's gaze and offered him a small smile.

He smiled back and returned his attention to the road. They had traveled until after the sunset and risen this morning before first light. They had made good progress. Better than Gwilim had hoped. The Lord was good.

They crested a rise and Gwilim reined the horse in. Both children stood and looked over his shoulders. In the distance, on another hill, pale army tents contrasted with the deep green of the Scottish landscape.

Gwilim swallowed hard as he carefully scanned for any identifiers of this army. Were they English or Scottish?

Movement caught his eye. Red fabric snapped in the breeze. Three yellow splotches stretched across it in three rows. He couldn't see them from here, but Gwilim knew they were the three golden lions on King Edward's flag. An English army. Far more dangerous for the children than a Scottish army would have been for him as a friar.

Gwilim glanced back at Isabelle. "It is probably best we don't go that way. Papers or no, there is no need to tempt fate."

Isabelle nodded and the children settled back down.

Gwilim turned the wagon to a forest trail. They had been too far away to see anyone. He prayed no one had seen them, either.

"He that dwelleth in the secret place of the most High shall abide under the shadow of the Almighty. I will say of the LORD, my refuge and my fortress: my God; in Him will I trust." The words of the psalms tumbled from Gwilim's lips in an endless prayer. The narrow path between the trees had him walking and leading the horse to assure the· wagon could pass. "Surely He shall deliver thee from the snare of the fowler—"

An English soldier entered the path ahead of them.

Gwilim's heart felt like it leapt into his throat and he struggled to breathe or swallow. He froze, and prayed the man would continue on without seeing them.

The soldier walked across the trail.

When he reached the midpoint, Gwilim dared a glance back at the children. They'd been eating, but now Isabelle waved her brother into the hiding spot.

Gwilim's lungs burned with his held breath.

The man stepped into the trees on the far side of the path.

The horse tossed his head, rattling the tack, and Gwilim thought he'd choke.

The soldier stepped back onto the path, stopped, and stared at him.

In a dozen quick strides, the Englishman was within a sword's reach. His greedy gaze swept over the wagon of crates. "Well, now, who might you be?" He slowly strolled around the wagon.

"Nobody you need concern yourself with at this time," Gwilim managed to say, though there was no moisture in his mouth.

The soldier stopped beside the wagon next to Gwilim, and a smirk rose on his lips. His gaze narrowed and he opened his mouth.

"Die, ya En'lish pig!" Henric leapt from his hiding place and raised his wooden sword.

The soldier's hand seized the hilt of his real weapon as he turned to the threat.

Gwilim swung his staff.

A resounding *thunk* echoed off the trees.

The soldier slumped to the ground and didn't move.

"Times change," Gwilim muttered. He was once a soldier. After his failure, he'd become a friar. Now, the situation demanded he be both. He could not fail.

He glanced up at Henric and snatched the wooden sword out of his hand. "You can have this back later." He nodded to Isabelle who poked her head out between the crates.

She grabbed hold of her brother and pulled him back inside.

Gwilim tossed the play sword under his seat and hurried to take up the horse's reigns before the fallen soldier woke.

He raised his gaze back to the trail and almost fainted away.

Five soldiers filled the path and stalked toward him.

"Lord, please," he whispered.

Chapter 45

Forest in Scotland

The pounding in Gwilim's head welcomed him back first. The aches in his body came next. He tried to bring his hand up to rub his head. When he couldn't, he realized the ache in his shoulders and the pain in his wrists were because his hands were bound behind his back.

He lifted his head and tried to figure out where he was and what had happened. Light from campfires to his left made him shut his eyes quickly. He turned his head the other way with a groan and tried again. The vision in his left eye was blurred and that eye barely opened.

He tried to wet his parched lips as he scanned the woods around him. He sucked in a breath at the sting as his tongue passed over a split in his lip and started it bleeding again. He wanted to spit the metal taste out of his mouth but he was sitting up with something bound behind him.

English soldiers were finishing their evening meal. The campfires glowing off their tents. The crates of the supplies he prepared to carry Isabelle and—

He jerked straighter. Isabelle and Henric! Where were the children?

The throb in his aching head increased as he scanned for them and tried to move.

Something slid across his back and he turned to glance over his right shoulder.

Isabelle looked up from red rimmed eyes.

Gwilim sighed heavily. "Are you all right, lass?" he whispered.

She nodded.

"They haven't hurt you?"

"Nay. Only ya."

"And your brother?"

Movement slid against his left shoulder and he turn to almost see the boy through his swollen eye. "Are you all right, lad?"

Henric nodded and leaned back against him.

Gwilim scanned the soldiers again. The crates were scattered around the wagon. He tested the rope around his wrists. His heart stuttered and his eyes filled with tears. The stinging around his swollen left eye only added to his growing discomfort.

"Lord, be my Redeemer this day," he whispered. His tears increased as memories of that horrid day blotted out the forest. "I cannot abide to fail my lord again. Not again," he cried, his stuttered breaths reminding him of the blows he'd taken to his ribs. As his tears increased, he raised his head to turn his face to the darkening sky above.

Movement arrested his prayer. A yellow shirt materialized out of the growing shadows. Gwilim had heard tales of the heavy saffron war-shirts, called leine croich, that Scottish warriors had worn into battle for centuries. He never expected to see one. None of the Scots he'd met dared reveal they were with the rebels in such a bold manner.

The bearded Scotsmen raised a finger to his lips as he stepped up behind the Englishman guarding Gwilim and the children. He wore a heavy leather jerkin over the long war-shirt but no mail to aid in his silent attack.

More saffron-clad warriors stepped from the trees.

The Englishman on guard duty turned, but before the man could raise the alarm, the rebel leader ran him through. Unfortunately, the falling body overturned the man's meal with a clatter that alerted the rest of the camp.

"Atta—" one soldier tried to yell before he was, likewise, cut down.

The rebels pulled burning branches from the fires and threw them on the tents.

Regulars ran out to escape the flames only to be impaled on rebel swords.

"Grab your weapons!" the English commander in the center of the camp yelled as he crossed swords with the rebel closest to him.

The English soldiers turned toward the trees to flee instead.

Isabelle and Henric trembled behind Gwilim, and tried to quiet their sobs.

Air hissed through Gwilim's lips as he turned his hands until he could grasp one of Isabelle's and one of Henric's. The children clung to him and he to them.

"Stand your ground," the commander ordered.

Any soldier who tried was cut down by a rebel blade.

"You Scottish bas—" An ax sunk deep into the commander's chest and he dropped to his back.

A few more death cries leaked out from the forest where the rebels chased down the last of the fleeing regulars. An eerie silence followed.

The children gripped his hands tighter.

As the rebels collected the English weapons, their leader strolled over to the body of the fallen commander and jerked his ax free. He turned and marched back toward Gwilim. Blood dripped from the blades of his sword and ax he held at his sides. "Ya be friend or foe?"

"Friar," Gwilim managed to say with his parched tongue.

The man smirked. "Good enough." He wiped his blades clean on the clothes of the first guard he'd killed, returned the ax to his belt, and turned.

Isabelle and Henric peeked out around Gwilim.

The rebel leader scowled. "So, the cowards hev stooped ta capturin' monks, lads, and lasses. We did them a favor by endin' their lives." He stepped forward, carefully slid his blade between them and cut their bindings.

He offered Gwilim a hand and hauled him to his feet.

Isabelle stepped close to Gwilim as Henric clung to her.

"Ya'd best come with us." The leader nodded to his men who had added their plunder to the crates they'd put back in the wagon, and waved Gwilim and the children to follow.

Isabelle glanced up at Gwilim. He took her hand with a smile and they walked beside the leader back into the forest.

Chapter 46

Forest in Scotland

Isabelle had finally stopped shaking. Henric walked a little behind her with some of the Scottish warriors who had rescued them. She stayed close to Gwilim as he told their leader, John Comyn, how they had been captured.

Light flickered through the dark trees as they came to another camp. This one was full of leine croich. York had a yellow war-shirt like theirs once. He'd burned it in front of Lord Sintest as a sign he wouldn't fight the man's rule over Din Osways.

Isabelle bumped into Gwilim as the men turned to look their way. These were her people, but they were warriors, and men. Would she ever feel safe?

Two women sat in the middle of the camp. The older one was a pretty lady with a light-blue dress and only a little gray in her hair. She stood with a gasp as they approached. The guard watching her stepped in her path before she could move forward toward them. His hand rested on the hilt of his sword. "Brother Gwilim?" she said.

The friar stopped talking and his mouth hung open.

John waved the guard away from the women.

The older one, who'd called the friar by name, came closer to them.

"What are you doing here?"

"My lady," Gwilim said at last. Excitement filled his voice and a smile turned his lips. "Oh, my Lord's blessings." He raised his hands high in the air and almost shouted. "Praise be His name."

"But why?" The lady's brows pinched tight together as she stared at Gwilim. "You should be with—"

"My lady," Gwilim interrupted. "There are many happenings to tell you. Lord Kenseth has sent me south—to be with *you*."

This was Lord Kenseth's wife—the one they were supposed to be going to so they would be safe. Isabelle glanced at Henric who had moved closer. He looked as confused as she felt. Why was the lady in Scotland and not in Conwy where they were supposed to be going?

"Us?" Lady Kenseth said.

Isabelle crept forward, and the pretty lady turned her kind brown eyes toward her. Small wrinkles formed at the corners of her eyes as she smiled.

"Pardon, my lady. This is Isabelle. The lad, Henric, is her brother." Gwilim waved her and Henric closer. "I believe this will explain." The friar pulled the letter from Lord Kenseth from his robe and handed to her.

The lady broke the red wax and unfolded the letter. As she read, the friar also explained.

"The young lass has served his lordship since his arrival."

The lady's eyes widened as she continued to read.

"There was a battle in their village," Gwilim said.

The lady's trembling fingers covered her mouth, but Isabelle couldn't tell if it was from what the friar said or what she read.

"Your husband is safe," Gwilim said quickly. "But many of the villagers lost their lives."

Isabelle swallowed her growing tears.

"Including these children's ..." Gwilim stopped as the lady finished the letter and looked up with tears rolling down her cheeks.

Isabelle glanced at Gwilim.

The friar stared and pursed his lips. "My lady?"

She thrust the letter back to him, and then dropped on her knees in front of Isabelle. She wrapped her arms around her so tightly Isabelle could feel the lady tremble as she cried. Again, Isabelle looked at Gwilim, but his eyes were on the letter.

"Oh my." He shook his head. "Dear Lord above ..." His eyes bulged as he continued to read. "This ..." He shook the letter. "This is not a letter of passage." He at last looked at Isabelle. "It is a letter of ... of *adoption*."

The lord had done more than just promise to protect them. He'd made them his family. Isabelle couldn't contain her own tears any longer. This woman clinging to her was now her muther. She wrapped her arms around her too and her tears increased.

Their new muther reached out for Henric.

He didn't move as he looked at her with his head tipped.

Isabelle reached for him with a smile drenched in tears.

He came at last and Muther wrapped one arm around him too.

They had a family again. Isabelle continued to cry as she remembered that Lord Kenseth had lost a son long ago. Now, he had a son and a daughter.

Muther looked up with a huge smile and brushed her hands over Isabelle and Henric's cheeks. "Welcome, my loves."

Gwendolyn introduced herself as she led them over to the other lady. "This is my maid, and friend, Katlyn." She brushed her hands over both their faces again. "Let's see about getting you two cleaned up. Are you hungry?"

Henric nodded vigorously.

Gwendolyn smiled. "All right. Food first, then we get you cleaned up." As they moved to where she had been when they arrived, her sweeping gaze washed over them. "I think, with a little adjusting, one of Katlyn's gowns could fit you, Isabelle."

Isabelle swiped at a new tear. Lady Gwendolyn already said her name with the love of a muther.

"You on the other hand, Henric, may be more of a challenge. There are not many squires among the rebels."

"I wanna leine croich," Henric said.

"No!" Isabelle almost shook.

Muther placed a comforting arm around her. "What a brave boy you are," Lady Gwendolyn's voice shook. "But for now, there is no reason to invite danger. There is enough of it for us already."

Katlyn returned with two plates and they sat on a fallen tree next to Lady Gwendolyn. She couldn't take her eyes off them and asked all about their lives as they ate.

Isabelle glanced around the rebel camp. No one, other than Gwilim, looked her way. He offered her a wide grin as he lifted his own plate in salute. She drew in her first real breath in days. Lord Kenseth—Da—had done right by them. Now, all they needed was for him to be safe and join them.

Chapter 47

Stirling, Scotland

Amersham straightened in his saddle as Governor de Warenne finally joined them. The chancellor had to send for someone to wake the governor as they took up lines against the Scots. Amersham couldn't believe their small number, which gathered north across Stirling bridge, and had come boldly clad in their saffron war-shirts.

Lieutenant Gandry, Lord Finon, and Captain Fenwick sat mounted before their large forces, on the south side of the bridge ready to crush the rebels who dared stand in the way of the king.

Amersham noted that Kenseth and his men had finally arrived. They took up position at the end of the long line of English and Scottish lords and their men.

"Report, Lieutenant," de Warenne said with a yawn.

"Ready, sir," Gandry replied.

Amersham kept looking down the line. "And Kenseth's troops?"

Without turning, Amersham could hear the smile in Gandry's voice. "Accounted for, my lord."

"Accounted for?" de Warenne said with a huff. "I suppose that is all we might expect."

"I know the men, sir." Gandry repositioned his horse so the governor could see him better. The man had ambition nearly as large as Amersham's. "They will fight."

Not to be outshined by the lieutenant, Amersham drew the governor's attention with a sharp snort. "As well they should."

"Excuse me, my lords," Richard Lundie, a Scotsman who had sided with Edward against his own, rode forward. "There is a wide ford less than half a league upstream where sixty men can easily cross. I can lead a contingent and we can flank the rebels, my lords."

"Governor de Warenne, there is no need for that." Amersham raised his hand toward the rebel forces they faced across the bridge. "There are few of them, and they won't even take up lines against us. We have proven it before. They are no match for English might."

Ignoring Lundie, de Warenne turned to Lord Finon. "This is your land, Finon. For the glory of the king and for England, let's make quick work of it. Soften them up."

As they had prearranged, Finon turned to Gandry, who turned to the flagman. "Archers!"

The flagman raised the crest full of bows and flying arrows.

A mass of archers stepped forward, arrows already nocked, and raised them.

"Fire!" de Warenne shouted.

Across the river, the rebels ducked safely behind their shields.

Angwyn sat astride his horse with his sword resting ready on his thigh. What was the governor thinking? The narrow bridge, which would only allow two to ride abreast, was the only way across to meet the enemy. This was a terrible place for battle. Whoever crossed first would be cut down before they made it to the other side.

He shook his head as he watched the English bows send fruitless arrows into the rebel shield wall.

In response, a small band of saffron war-shirts raced to the river's edge, but their bows were no match for those that the English fired. Kenseth and his men didn't even bother to move as the arrows fell to the ground almost five-feet away.

Ramonth rode up.

Angwyn kept his gaze on the battlefield. "This is madness."

"It will be short," Ramonth said with great excitement.

Angwyn raised and pointed his sword across the river. "They have the advantage!"

Ramonth shrugged. "They can't even reach us. I'm fine with just sitting here all day."

The Scottish archers scurried back to their cover as the English released another volley.

Angwyn shook his head again. This had to be the most ill-conceived battle plan ever. Had de Warenne lost his faculties?

"That is enough," de Warenne said with a huff. No doubt he worried over the cost of the arrows.

"My lord?" Gandry was confused too.

The governor turned and looked at Amersham. "Let's finish this, chancellor." He nodded and yawned again. "Let Din Osways have the honor."

Gandry nearly leapt from his horse. "With pleasure, my lord." He turned to the flagman again. "Raise the flag."

The yellow crest with three boars' heads rose high in the air.

"The flag is raised." Ramonth pointed to the Din Osways crest flying over the governor's head.

Angwyn followed his line of sight but what he saw was Gandry, grinning madly between the governor and the king's chancellor. "In the name of all that is holy, this is not right." Angwyn wasn't only thinking about the justice of trying to conquer these people. His men were the furthest contingent from the bridge, and the bridge was the worst place to cross.

Ramonth leaned in the saddle toward him and shouted. "Our flag is raised. Damn you and your God." He turned his horse and called to the men. "Men of Din Osways!" He raised his sword in the air. "For glory of our king!"

The men cheered, but Angwyn positioned his horse in their path. Fallen arrows snapped under his horse's hooves.

"Hold! Hold your place." Angwyn turned to Ramonth, his captain, his friend, a man that now looked on him with the same hatred of Orion and Alistair. "I did not fight my way from Wales to Scotland to sacrifice myself, or *my* men, on this field."

"We have our orders!"

Angwyn's heart thrummed in an erratic rhythm. This was not an honorable battle; this was to be a slaughter of him and his men. He had to make Ramonth see.

Amersham looked down the line as Kenseth and his captain, Ramonth, argued.

"Raise it again," de Warenne ordered.

The flagman lowered the Din Osways crest and rose it again, giving the long pole it perched on a quick swing so the banner waved to catch their attention.

The lord and his captain were still locked in their debate. If they couldn't get Kenseth to the battlefield and quickly, all Amersham's plans would be for naught.

The governor huffed. "Finon! Fenwick! Send your men." His arm pointed down the line. "Amersham, take care of that."

Amersham noted the shock in the two men's faces, but eagerly turned his attention back to Kenseth. "My honor, sir." If Amersham couldn't get Kenseth to the battlefield, he'd bring the battle to him.

The Stirling flag and that of Fenwick's men was raised and a loud shout filled the south side of the river.

The trusty English regulars charged for the bridge.

Chapter 48

Stirling, Scotland

Ramonth watched their flag raise again. He'd taken a knee before de Warenne years ago. He'd sworn his sword to king Edward. To refuse to go into battle when called would mean death. He stared at Kenseth, his once friend. The man was afraid to fight. Well, he was not. "They raise our flag again."

Kenseth looked, but it was as if he didn't see the truth and they needed to act now—decisively.

Ramonth settled the matter within himself. He would break his oath with the lesser man for the glory of serving the greater one. Who knew, when they won this battle in a few hours, if de Warenne might grant him Din Osways or even greater holdings?

Two other flags were raised and those contingents leapt to the battle with great shouts.

"Dear God," Kenseth muttered.

If Ramonth didn't act soon, the glory would go to another. He turned his rage on his former friend. "Damn you, and your God," he said again.

Ramonth turned to *his* men. They had already said they'd follow him. "Men of Din Osways, on me! To glory for our king!"

Ramonth led the charge for the bridge, almost crashing his mount into Kenseth's as he raced past. This was it. This was his moment to be his own man and get the honor due him for all he had endured.

He was forced to slow as the line of men and horses struggled to fit on the narrow bridge, but the Scots hadn't moved. They would be across soon and show those yellow-shirts the power of English steel.

Angwyn watch Ramonth lead all of Sintest's men to the bridge. Their crossing was hampered by all those already on the bridge, and the Scottish archers loosed more of their arrows into those crossing.

Angwyn had not only lost his captain, and the English soldiers he never gained rule over, but a third of his own men had joined his former friend—to their deaths, Angwyn was sure.

Movement to his left drew his attention. The chancellor rode toward him and the men he had left. "Kenseth!" the slender man roared with his sword leveled as his horse collided with Angwyn's. "I shall have your head!"

Angwyn blocked the death blow, and shoved the threatening sword away. The man was not made for battle. Add to that he'd never met the chancellor, and Angwyn couldn't understand the man's rage. "You have us all doomed!"

Their two mounts circled one another.

"You were to be first, Kenseth."

Theirs swords crashed together before Angwyn could ask why.

"Why can't you and your infernal wife not do as you are told—" Amersham slashed "and die."

Angwyn ducked under the blow that would have taken his head. "What have you done to Gwendolyn?"

"Given her to the king." Amersham laughed as he thrust again at Angwyn's chest.

Another third of his Welsh soldiers rode away to join Ramonth.

He was being deserted on every side and betrayed. This command had not been about restoring his honor. He'd been set up to fail from the very beginning. *Dear God, help me.*

As if hearing his thoughts, Amersham slashed at him and said, "You made it so easy."

Finon's men made it across the bridge as the yellow-shirt archers fled before them.

All but one.

The yellow-shirt with a full red beard drew back his bow.

The arrow fired. Amersham's horse stepped to the side and broke one of the earlier arrows. Amersham was in the kill zone. Kenseth bolted forward. Amersham braced against what he must have assumed was a charge.

The arrow imbedded in Amersham's neck, easily finding the opening above his mail. He might have been saved if he'd been wearing his helmet. He slumped forward into Angwyn. The arrow protruded from him as his sword dropped to the ground from his limp hand.

Angwyn held the dead man as his gaze returned to the battle. Finon's men and Fenwick with his men were across the bridge. Almost two thousand men, by Angwyn's count.

He released Amersham and the man's body fell to the ground.

A roar erupted from the Scottish lines and hundreds of spearmen charged out of the forest from the high ground and attacked the horsemen in the front.

Movement on his left drew Angwyn's attention again. Gandry drew his sword with a shout and led a dozen regulars down the line straight at him.

The last of Angwyn's men saw the charge too. "My lord!" They surged forward to meet Gandry and his men.

The clash of swords between Gandry's men and those loyal to Angwyn was drowned out by the Scots as they moved to the English foot soldiers behind the king's fallen mounted men.

"You have been betrayed," Eudav, on of his faithful men, said as he rode up beside Angwyn.

With his sword still at his side, Angwyn watched his last dozen men engage Gandry.

But his gaze was drawn back to the battle that was playing out just as he'd feared. The English had nowhere to go. Scots before them and their own men clogging their only retreat, they were trapped.

He spotted Ramonth at the far end of the bridge. Sword raised, he tried to hack his way across. An arrow drove into his chest. And another. Ramonth's horse stumbled, and his body fell off into the river.

Angwyn watch his friend disappear below the surface. "Lord have mercy on his soul."

"My lord!" Eudav cried.

Angwyn's head snapped around to the battle before him against those who claimed the same loyalty.

One of his men fell from Gandry's blade.

Others regulars and their lords, lined up waiting to join the battle, turn their attention on Angwyn's small remaining band. They were itching to join the fight, and if they couldn't get to the Scot's, it seemed Angwyn and his men were the next best target. Several small contingents advanced toward them from the English lines.

"We must flee," Eudav said.

Angwyn whirled his horse with his last three mounted warriors and raced away from the battlefield.

Chapter 49

Scottish Forest

A branch slapped Angwyn in the face as he fled through the forest. He ducked under the next low branch. Eudav and the last two of his soldiers careened through the thick trees beside him.

With the way clear for several strides, he glanced back. Gandry pointed his sword and shouted something Angwyn couldn't understand from the distance, the noise he and his men were making, and the pounding of his heart in his ears.

'You've been betrayed.' Eudav's words thundered in his head. Gandry had restored—no improved—his standing in order to assure Angwyn fell.

His horse leapt between two trees. But they had been too close together for him to clear. Bark scraped across his left thigh, removing fabric and flesh.

Amersham's words flared in his mind as he dodged another branch. "Why can't you and your wife do as you are told—and die."

Angwyn straightened only for a small branch to smash into his head. Without his helmet, the rough wood tore across his face and cut a gash across his nose and cheek. Blood dripped from his jaw. He thrust his pain aside as he thought of his beloved wife. "Please, Lord. I know I don't deserve Your mercy, but Gwendolyn … Please let her be all right."

Even above all the noise he and men were creating, and Grandy's men in their pursuit, Angwyn could still hear the roar of the battle. A righteous battle of the Scots defending their homes and families. The right to live without being cut down in the street by invaders.

The English fought to get more. More land. More women to abuse. More wealth. More. He'd been so wrong to bend a knee to Edward.

Isabelle came to mind. He'd made her his daughter. If he hadn't taken a knee after William's death, Gandry and his men would have destroyed her. Isabelle and Henric were safe because of him.

They burst from the woods onto a wide road. It had taken most of the day to move his contingent of seventy-four men from Din Osways to Stirling. But, then, he'd led mostly foot soldiers and a couple of wagons for the tents and food.

Now, he only had three mounted men with him. All that was left of his proud fighting men. Men he knew by name and cared about. Not to mention those of Sintest's men who had never been his.

There was no sound of the chase behind them.

"My lord?" Eudav said through hard pants of breath.

If they turned toward home, it would take a week. The horse under him couldn't run that long. Was Gwendolyn safe? How did he protect her? Amersham was dead—but he'd said he 'gave her' to the king. What did that even mean?

"Lord Kenseth?" Eudav shouted.

"We can reach Din Osways in a couple of hours if we push the horses. It might be the only place we can find safe harbor at this point."

Eudav nodded. "We are with you, my lord."

"Kenseth, you will pay!" Gandry's rage echoed from the trees.

They spurred their horses to speed again and charged down the road, cutting through the forest to save time wherever they could.

Their horses were covered in lather as they came to the place Gwilim's wagon had become mired in the mud. The ruts from that day were dried in the uneven road surface now.

"My lord, we must rest the horses."

He hadn't caught sight of Gandry and his men, but he felt their pursuit as a growing danger that wouldn't let his heart slow. "They will not, so we cannot. We must reach Din Osways if there is to be any hope at all."

They renewed the hard charge as the horses strained to maintain the pace.

Either they would reach the protective gates and the faithful men they had left behind in time or they wouldn't. What kept rattling in Angwyn's head was Gwendolyn and the children.

If, like Amersham had said, she was part of the court now … If the king did "have her" … What did that mean for the children? How could he get Gwendolyn back? Did she still want him?

Again, his only option from so far away when he didn't know what was truth and what was lie, was prayer. God had to be his answer. Would the Lord even still listen to his prayers?

They crested the rise and, as they had a few months ago, looked down on Din Osways and the village. All was quiet. In this corner of Scotland, there was a measure of peace.

The horses heaved and trembled under them.

Almost there.

A battle cry split the air, sending birds squawking into the skies and woodland creatures scurrying through the brush. Gandry and his men charged up the road behind him.

"To the gates, men." Angwyn kicked his horse to flee, but the animal stumbled.

Chapter 50

Din Osways village

Angwyn and his last three warriors charged down the hill toward the village and the keep of Din Osways on the other side, far too slow.

Angwyn's horse stumbled again. The animal was near dead.

They neared the village. After what the English had done, and Angwyn had been helpless to prevent, he knew he'd find no safety there.

His horse staggered and Angwyn was pitched from the saddle. The animal took a few more faltering steps before he went down.

Eudav and the other two with him turn to face Gandry. Three against ten, his men had no chance and each fell dead on the road. So close to safety—yet in this land it is seldom found.

With Angwyn's men dead, there was nothing standing between the former guard and him.

Gandry and his men dismounted. He drew his sword with a cocky smile.

Angwyn gained his feet and drew his blade too. He had no chance against ten men. But he would take Gandry down if he could.

"You aren't that good," Gandry said.

"But at least I can kill *you*." Angwyn scanned the surroundings. Did Hywel and the men he'd left in the keep see what was happening? Could they rally a defense fast enough?

Noise caused Angwyn to glance over his shoulder. The villagers, men and women, stepped from the village onto the road. They marched toward Angwyn with pitchforks, sickles, axes, rolling pins, hammers, and anything else they could find.

Angwyn steeled himself. "Lord, I know I don't deserve it, but have mercy on my soul. I have failed in so many ways ..." He swallowed and waited to see if the first blow would come from the villagers, or the former guard. "Please, protect Gwendolyn and the children where I could not. And ... forgive me, Lord."

"This should be fun." Gandry continued to laugh.

What looked like every adult remaining in the village stepped up beside and behind Angwyn and stopped. They stared down Gandry *with* Angwyn.

Gandry chuckled. "*This* is your army now? And you call yourself a *noble.*" The last word spit out of his mouth.

And there it was. He been offered nobility by a man he didn't like or respect. He'd thought it was all he needed to feel whole again. But the restoration of his soul had nothing to do with titles or position.

Angwyn tightened his grip on his hilt and smiled. "If you are what they call nobility ..." He thrust his weapon in the air with his shout. "Then I. Choose. Scotland!"

The villagers roared to his battle cry.

Gandry narrowed is gaze and leveled his weapon. "Then, in Scotland you shall remain."

"Lord Kenseth has long ago made his provision to meet his Maker!" a familiar voice shouted.

Everyone looked up and Gandry turned to see Gwilim on the rise behind him. He stood in a wide stance with his staff planted in the ground next to him.

What in earth was the man doing here? He couldn't have delivered the children already. Where were they?

Gwilim pointed his staff at Gandry. "What about you?"

A growl emanated from the former guard. "Oh, I shall provide. I shall provide my wrath and my vengeance. I shall provide what man has wrought, beginning with you!" He raised his weapon to attack the friar with a fearsome roar. It was cut off in a strangled cry as Angwyn charged forward and thrust his sword through the man. His body slid off Angwyn's blade and dropped to the soft dirt.

Gwilim gave Angwyn a smug nod. "The Lord provides."

The English soldiers' gazes shifted from their fallen leader to Angwyn.

Angwyn tensed, ready for the first to swing at him, but their gazes shifted again and they dropped their weapons.

"That He does," a deep voice said from behind Angwyn.

He turned to see a broad-chested, yellow-clad warrior with a trimmed beard behind him. More saffron shirts emerged from the woods, and the villagers sang out with a battle cry. The rebels answered in kind, until the village road shook with their sound.

Angwyn's sword hung heavy at his side. It would seem he'd been saved. He staggered. Two villagers caught him and steadied him. They'd come to his defense. After what they had suffered. They'd chosen to fight *with* him.

The rebels shuffled about until a path formed between their members. There in the gap were well-dressed women. Not any women. His dear Gwendolyn, her maid Katlyn, and Isabelle. Henric was there too.

Isabelle led the charge as she lifted her gown and raced toward him. Gwendolyn was not far behind.

As they approached, Angwyn tried to find his balance and step forward but his strength failed him. He fell into Gwendolyn's arms. "Oh, my love."

She cradled his face and stared for a moment. A smile grew and she leaned in to kiss him. He tightened his arms around her. This—this was honor. This was home. His lovely wife. These children. These people.

As Gwendolyn pulled from him, Isabelle hugged him too. Yes, he had found what he was looking for in far-off Scotland.

Henric marched forward with his wooden sword drawn and pointing at Angwyn. He turned the play weapon to hold it in both hands, stepped in front of Angwyn and laid it at his feet before he stepped back, bowed, and then offered him a Scottish salute.

Angwyn smiled. "Well met, son. Well met."

Activity swirled around him as the rebels secured the English prisoners. Hywel and his men charged up.

Angwyn's heart filled with such gratitude, he took Gwendolyn's soft hand in his and lowered to his knees. She joined him as he bowed his head. "Thank you, Lord," he muttered in awe.

"Lord God Almighty," Gwilim's strong voice called above the noise. His hands rose toward the sky. "We give You all the praise …"

Angwyn glanced at Gwendolyn, Isabelle, and Henric. He brushed his hand over Henric's head, then he squeezed Isabelle's hand. Finally, he kissed Gwendolyn again. "Welcome home," he said with a smile.

About the Author

Michelle Janene (Murray) is a multi-published author
who works part-time in her church's office
and blissfully exists in the creations of her mind as she writes in
a wide range of genres.
She lives with two crazy dogs and the characters of her
imagination.

If you enjoyed *The Last Good King* please review it on your
favorite site.

Join Michelle's email list and get a free novelette at
MichelleJanene.com
You can also connect with Michelle on:
Facebook: Michelle Janene-Author or Strong Tower Press
Twitter: @MichelleJaneneM
Instagram: michellejanene_author
Pinterest: www.pinterest.com/michellejanene
Goodreads: Michelle Janene
StrongTowerPress.com

About the Screenwriter

David M. Hyde, is a multi-optioned award-winning screenwriter most recently co-writing a 9/11 docu-drama for Carolyn Mack Productions and is a limited-series writer for the Al Turner Company.

Writing his whole life, David has focused specifically on screenwriting most recently. David Has written or co-written a total of seven screenplays and episodic scripts for one limited series as well as being a script consultant for countless other projects. David lives in Northern California, enjoying family, the outdoors and, of course, a really good story.

Other Books

Check out these books also by Michelle

Mission: Mistaken Identity

The Changed Heart Series:
God's Rebel
Rebel's Son
Hidden Rebel

Seer of Windmere

Barbarian Hero

Guardians of Truth

Culling a Miracle

Savior Stones Chronicles
Lost Stones

Found in the Scars

Made in the USA
Las Vegas, NV
27 February 2022

44688880R00128